BLOOD LEGENDS

ASCENSION

KIM PETERSEN

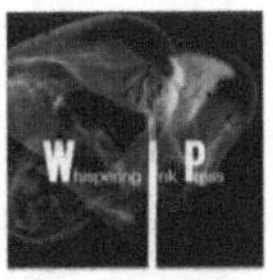

BLOOD LEGENDS

ASCENSION

USA Today Bestselling Author

KIM PETERSEN

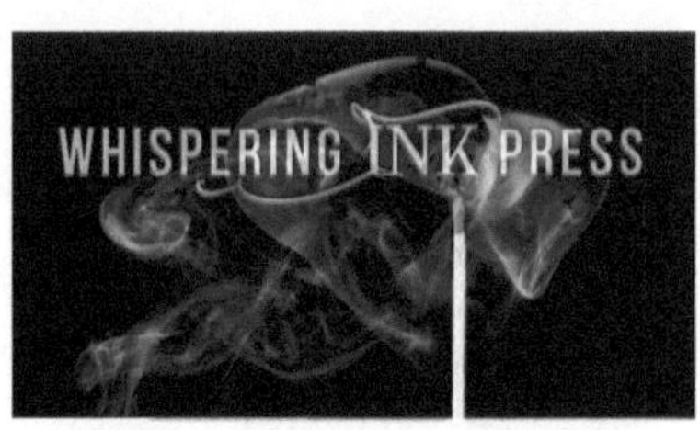

eBook IBSN: 978-0-6489305-0-1

Paperback IBSN: 978-0-6489305-1-8

Edited by Paul Vander Loos

Cover & Formatting by Paradox Book Covers

WITH THANKS TO...

Beth Prentice, Paul Vander-Loos, Patti Roberts, Harley
Christensen, and Xavier Eastenbrick.
With special thanks to Joseph Nassise.

CONTENTS

DISTRICT HUMAN

They call it Bloodfaye. I call it a perpetual fire on earth where the wicked are punished after death. That might sound like an exaggeration on my part. It wasn't. It was a forged existence. Nothing shone other than the silver egg that hovered above us like a deceptive halo. Imitation did nothing to appease a restless soul. It was the new kindred way of life.

I rubbed the back of my neck. My muscles ached from endless days working the laboratory. Today was no different. Bloodfaye was open for business. Humans had to pass a blood test before they were permitted into the dome city where they were promised a better life.

It was a sham. We took their blood for two reasons:

1. Contaminated blood could potentially kill a vampire if consumed.

2. The search for the invincible and elusive AB
    positive blood was as eternal as life after
    death.

The fact that I possessed a vial of gold mixed with Lygarou blood was a delicate situation, but I wasn't losing any sleep over it. As it was, Melissa was currently taking care of all matters sleep deprivation. The woman was haunting me. She had been my wife and Avila's mom. The last time I'd seen her was the morning she had left the house to go for her usual run. It was the same day she had died.

I frowned and pushed those thoughts aside as the beginnings of a commotion erupted from across the lab. It was the usual lab set-up – lengthy benchtops, glassed cubicles and an array of scientific machines. Marius was a resourceful overlord. I peered through the white coats skimming the room. They stunk like self-importance, and dotted between them were the Leavings who were ushered through the lab faster than a Sushi conveyer belt.

"Hold still, Leaving!"

The brash order was issued by some vampire kid they'd dumped in the laboratory and called a Mysticus scientist. There were dozens of them. Most of them couldn't distinguish a fart from a turd, let alone competently take the blood of incoming Leavings. I had no choice but to deal with it.

Mongrel blood.

I cursed and stood up from my workstation. Some vampires were like foul gutters. This one was poking a Leaving woman in a rather offensive fashion. Time to intervene. I'd been here before. It was the barbaric vampire guttersnipes who lost their shit often. An event that inevitably resulted in a dead human.

"I said, stop fricken squirming bitch!"

I picked up my pace. The woman whimpered. I had a zero-dead human policy on my watch. They all knew it but not all of them had the ability to care when confronted by human blood and frustration.

The woman cried out as I approached. Her limp hair hung over grotty features like rotten seaweed. Her stench resembled the muck too. They seriously needed to do something about the hygiene of Leavings, preferably before they reached the lab for their mandatory blood testing.

I stopped behind him. His name was lost on me. They should consider issuing name tags too.

"Easy, kid. She's not a dartboard."

"Her veins are rolling or something!"

I peered at the underside of her arm. Her skin was angry-red and swollen.

"Small veins. Perhaps we should choose a butterfly needle and attempt on her other arm."

The dumbass didn't even look me as he gave a frustrated hiss before tightening his grip on her wrist. The syringe poised briefly. Her dull eyes glanced at me; her pasty lips trembled as he jabbed the needle into her flesh. He didn't appear to be aiming for anything. She shrieked and jerked her arm. *Blood fountain.* He hit it and it was suddenly spurting everywhere. She wailed louder. I groaned. His lips stretched to bare his fangs. A growl followed before he went to lunge for her. I stopped him by grabbing a fistful of his ginger hair in the nick of time.

Mongrel. Blood.

"How bestial of you." I gave a growl of my own and yanked him clear off his chair. He landed on the floor and promptly scrambled to his haunches. His eyes flashed and he hissed at me. *Life just gets better ... and better.* I gave him a twisted grin and studied my talons. "Ah, and so he challenges me to a dual-dance ... vampire trout must be in the mood for a second death today, hmm?"

His brows instantly lowered as he started to back away. I expected as much, but my problems were far from over. I had a lab teaming with vampires and a Leaving who may as well have had an *"all you can eat"* sign plastered on her head. The air was now thick with the scent of hunger. They were stalking all around. Eyes like neon beads. Breath like hot alley cats.

"Back away, vampires!" The warning went unheard. I grabbed the nearest roll of cotton and pressed it against the woman's now overactive vein. He butchered her good for a rooky armed with only a thin needle. A low hiss emanated from behind. The woman screamed.

Shit. Fear elevated a vampire's insatiable desire for blood.

"Keep still and shut up." I gripped her wrist and scrambled among the empty vials, packages of syringes and antiseptic bottles splayed over the benchtop for some tape. It remained unfound and my heart thundered. The crusniks were closing in.

The woman skittered closer to me. I shoved her behind me, and she grappled at my lab coat as a female vampire with pink bangs and studded nostrils displayed her fangs. Talons twisted at the ends of her hair. Nostrils like a flame. Others inched closer, transfixed by the promise of fresh blood for the taking. Jaws salivated as they sought out the woman. *Meat market fair.* I needed backup.

Luckily there were guards and Shadow Guardians stationed in the lab for incidents like this. *Where the hell are they when you need them?* I gave the blood-lusting creatures my most hideous growl as some guards began pushing through the growing mob. *Finally.* Relief was in sight. It was Michal's shrill voice rising above pulsating hisses that caught my attention next.

"Coming through! Coming through!"

He emerged from among the throng of vamps with a few guards at his side, stopping abruptly when he copped sight of me and the woman nearly pushed up against the benchtop. Brown eyes blinked rapidly over her splattered blood as he made tittering noises. His fidgety thumbs probed his glasses.

"What in the name is this mess?"

The guards began ushering the predators away. Some of them resisted. They hissed and growled like feral animals. I ignored them and gazed toward the blood that doused the benchtop and floor.

"It's called blood, Michal. It's what we do here, remember?"

He gave me a filthy look. "How they expect us to work like this is beyond me!"

"Understatement of the century." I pushed the woman toward him. "Wrap her up properly and give her a pass."

His jaw dropped. Guards began shouting. A few of the mongrel bloods were getting feistier. The tension was brewing – just perfect

"A pass? B … but, master … she hasn't been cleared for District H."

I gave a tight smile. "She has now. Shall we use this current turn of events and escort the Leaving out of here?"

His lips parted. Spittle dribbled out of his mouth before he clamped his mouth shut and nodded. *Ding, ding.* He understood.

"Grab what you can," I said.

It was tedious smuggling items from the laboratory. Marius had guards assigned around the clock which had forced us to set up our own makeshift lab to work the hybrid blood. We'd chosen a discreet hub in the underground subway located along the wall that separated the districts in the far reaches of District H. It was better than nothing.

Michal fussed over the Leaving woman; he secured her wound tight while offering a running rant. "It's going to be okay, Leaving woman. We just have to ensure the bloodsuckers on the other side won't detect your fresh wound so easily… This will help you avoid the soowoo tooth fairy if you know what I mean."

"H - huh?"

She was terrified. I had to look away. Her life wasn't about to improve any time soon, but that was out my hands. I didn't run the joint.

Humans had become our bona fide blood-cows. If they passed their bloods, they were allocated quarters in District H – the human section of Bloodfaye. They were enslaved after that. Bloodfaye had a no free-loader policy, a fact I found ironic considering each Leaving was eloquently drained of blood every eight weeks to appease the clan's thirst. Most of them survived the periodic bloodletting.

Life beneath the dome was a far cry from the vision Marius had painted. Granted, the entire process was still in its infancy. There was much to establish as far as procedures and regulations were concerned. No time to think about that right now. Michal and I were just about ready to begin a process of our own.

I glanced at the guards on crowd control. The baking coven were still restless, but I knew the distraction wouldn't last.

"Hurry up!" It was a grunt issued at Michal as he carefully wrapped a few basic laboratory apparatuses in a white cloth – things like test tubes, tongs and funnels. I stuffed a pair of goggles, clamps and a few droppers into my pockets before encircling an arm around the trembling woman.

"Come on, love. Let's get you through to District H."

A handful of Shadow Guardians stood around the exit door. One of them was Lena – the tall, leathery Latino who had accompanied me part the way into wolf-mission wilderness some time ago. She had taken to me since my return. I was reluctant to admit that the feeling was mutual. Her dark roots dipped with her curt nod.

"Master Jett." Chaffed lips grinned as she moved away from her peers and pushed open the door. "I see you're leaving at just the right moment this afternoon."

I gently shoved the Leaving woman across the threshold after Michal. "Hello Lena. As usual, your observation skills impress and delight."

Her eyes scanned my bulging pockets before flitting up to me. She flicked her chin and stepped closer. "Master Zaros was spotted wandering through District H earlier."

"And?"

Zaros was a fluctuating version of Marius; an

overlord vampire. He was erratic and conniving. His desire for power made him extremely dangerous. I liked him as much as the vile aftertaste of a lowlife hawker.

"I saw him heading toward the old subway. He wasn't alone."

I squared my jaw. "Thank you, Lena."

She smiled and stepped back, sweeping her arm toward the door. "Good day, master Jett."

"And to you."

I walked from the lab with my pockets intact. The sounds of hyped hisses and growling guards were muffled beyond the closing door. I possessed many things of value in my pockets these days. None so much as the few members of my own secret sector.

2

STREETS WITH NO NAMES

Graphene and silicon wafers. The brittle crystalline solid filled many of the latticed gaps in the world's strongest most pliable material to create a humongous solar panel. *Lifeforce.* It was one big breathable UV protective heating pad; a fact I found pleasing considering my blood ran like the Arctic ocean. It was shaded like the moon and flexed slightly over the city like a futuristic hub generating Bloodfaye's power. I didn't know how Marius had managed to score so much of the innovative material that made the dome. It was damned genius.

Michal's feet did double time beside me as we strode through District H. We'd left the Leaving woman in the capable hands of Sun. She was one of the very few I trusted in the new world and happened to be handling the Leavings' lodgings that afternoon. The District reeked like rotten vegetables, human waste and stale sweat. They were still ironing out the ventilation and sewerage systems. They'd tapped into the city's main water supply. The water was clean and drinkable for our captives, albeit sewage was another matter altogether. I wasn't a plumber but I looked forward to cleaner air when visiting District H. Although, the district's living conditions weren't high on Marius' to-do list. He currently had more pressing matters to occupy his mind. Like establishing the reign of vampires in the new world.

The thought caused my gut to clench. I refocused. We were headed for the subway at the back of the city. I walked briskly through the dirty streets, barely seeing the small groups of Leavings lingering in the entrances of old brownstones and aging apartment buildings. They appeared desperate and somber. The vibe was desolate; the sky a silver moon promising nothing but a wasteland. Soon, it would become black with nightfall and the promise of death.

I caught sight of an elderly man sprawling on the dead grass along the sidewalk. His brown patched sweater swallowed his frail frame and he was motionless. He was barely alive and he was guard bait. Michal voiced my thoughts.

"Deplorable."

"Agreed."

"Then why don't you make a suggestion to Marius about the treatment of these Leavings?" He waved an arm toward the old man. "Surely his affection for Avila puts you in a position of influence? Elderly people are in no shape to undergo the bloodletting cycles."

I grimaced. "An overlord's affection for my daughter does not influence make, particularly when such suggestions serve no purpose in his agenda for power."

"Good point, though someone once said it was wise to keep your friends close and your enemies closer."

"Now we're using old-world clichés?" The thought of keeping close council with Marius made my skin crawl. "Look around, Michal, our overlord is too busy thriving on his own reflection, let alone his love for vampirism. There is no place for old-world thinking here. It wouldn't take a vampire genius to sniff out the wolf among the sheep when he comes calling."

He smirked. "Nice one." He was referring to my wolf pun. We were, after all, the keepers of such precious hybrid blood. He swallowed hard and glanced at me. "You know that you are in a position of power to help improve the living conditions in District H, at least until we can restore humanity with a cure for the V-virus."

"I know nothing of the sort. Besides, Marius listens to no one but himself, that I do know."

He huffed. "Takes one to know one."

I ignored his remark and glanced at him. He clutched the lab supplies against his chest and blinked rapidly. He did that a lot lately. His features were pinched beneath a layer of beaded sweat. He looked like a flushed ferret on a mouse wheel.

He looked back at me with annoyance. "What?"

"Nothing."

I looked away and deliberately picked up my pace. He knew how I felt about Marius favoring the affections of Avila. It bothered me to no end. There were hundreds of female vampires who occupied space in District V, and the shrewd overlord had a thing for *my* daughter. I didn't want to think about it.

Michal panted. He was falling behind. "Can we go any faster, *master*?"

I grinned. "I can go *a lot* faster, how about you?"

"I could if you'd turn me."

"Not happening today."

"When then?"

Never.

Michal was the only human other than the Shadow Guardians to remain off limits to vampires and the bloodletting program. He was fortunate and yet he wanted nothing more than to be kindred. Go figure. Marius refused to turn him and had forbid others to initiate the transition. Perhaps it was his fondness for the neurotic little man that compelled his reasoning. I didn't know, but his eternal death wasn't going to be on my hands.

I avoided an answer and gestured toward a group of

Mysticus guards up ahead. "Let's just focus on the matter at hand, shall we?"

"Y ... yep!"

Arrogance. It was a pungent fume and one I'd grown accustomed to since my passage into vampirism. Most kindred naturally adopted a superior attitude upon turning. Even the greatest of egotists in the old world had nothing on this lot. Supernatural ability bred conceit. They thought they were invincible. I longed for the day to prove them otherwise.

My eyes narrowed on four male guards as we approached. They all wore the same getup – white leather and chunky black boots adorned with silver buckles. Thin white gloves concealed bony hands while dark glasses shaded their eyes as they bantered back and forth.

Impudence.

I had it nailed and adopted my most courtly pose as I gave them a nod. I could play the game. Decorum was second trait. As a master, it was expected of me. "Good day, gentlemen."

They gave a hasty greeting. Pale skin gleamed as luminous as their lustrous hair. Vampires were glazed and polished creatures. Even the most gnarly variety. One of them stopped walking and eyed the bundle Michal clenched against his chest possessively. He gestured toward the bulky wrap.

"What have you there, Leaving?"

Michal stiffened.

"N … nothing."

"Na … na … nothing?" He laughed as his goons halted beside him. "Looks like something to me."

Wizpire lightbulbs ensued.

"Yeah, what's with the parcel? Have the contents been cleared?"

Cowboys. My nerves bristled. I groaned inwardly as one of them moved closer to Michal. Hair like liquorice contrasted against white-leathered shoulders. Lips like gills twisted. "Answer the question Leaving."

Michal jerked. His eyes widened beneath his spectacles; tremulous fingers tightened around the bundle as I stepped in front of him. I tilted my head and deadpanned the guard. "You dare question a Leaving accompanying a master?"

Golden eyes penetrated dark shades. "As Mysticus guards it is our business to investigate all suspicious behavior in District H."

Calm. My temples throbbed. "He carries supplies requested by Zaros who is currently in the district awaiting our special delivery." I forced a smile and motioned behind me. "We are here in service to our overlord. Is our behavior more suspicious than the Leaving I spotted rolling on the street back there?"

He was silent for a beat and his gaze followed my gesture. "A sponge?"

"It would seem."

He nodded. "Thank you, master Jett. Our apologies for disrupting your path."

"Apology accepted." I moved closer. "You'd do well to remember that this Leaving plays an important role in the progression of Bloodfaye's scientific arena. He is vital to your masters and as such, you will treat him respectfully at all times. Do you understand, vampire?"

His goon peeps cackled behind him as they started to move away.

"Come on, Ty, let's go investigate the *real* suspicious behavior."

The cowboy said nothing more. His eyes flashed and the veins beneath his chin became magenta vines as he gave a fast nod and walked away. The cords in my neck twanged. I didn't dwell. Michal gasped loudly as we set off again.

"I … I cannot believe you!"

We took the final corner. The road stretched along the tall iron-meshed wall separating the districts. Brownstone dwellings gave way to an industrial scene. Broken windows and patchwork doors garnished the worn exterior of warehouses and outlet buildings. The streets were quieter in this section of the city.

I kept my gaze ahead. "What?"

His voice was fretful. "Pointing out that poor Leaving man back there. They'll cause him more harm and enjoy every moment. You should be ashamed!"

"Ashamed is allowing your cover to be blown,

Michal." I glanced at him. "That man was already dead; you are not. Do you realize what they will do to you should they discover your part in our little running experiment?"

"Y … yes, they'll kill me."

"Not before they tie you to a post and slowly remove bits of skin and limbs one by one. Death by a thousand cuts – sound appealing?"

"N … nope!"

"I didn't think so." I slowed down as we approached the subway. The hairs on my arms stiffened as my gaze settled on the overhanging sign above the entrance. *Crata Village* – the smoke-stacked stop in the old world. The air stifled against my lungs and my ears pricked with the sound of a dull scream emanating from below street level.

Zaros. He and his crew must be in the underground tunnels. A rarity. Those subway passages were usually barren of life and the reason we had selected the site as our science hub in the first place. I motioned toward the doorway of the building near us. The dwelling appeared uninhabited and would provide a suitable space to stow Michal while I checked it out. "Stay here until I return."

He didn't argue. I ushered him through the door, briefly scanning a vast room filled with timber work benches, half-dressed mannequins and other unusual props. Rolls of fabric and industrial sewing machines covered in thick dust occupied the tables. I emptied my pockets.

His snuff-colored eyes blinked at me. "What if they discovered the lab?"

"Unlikely."

We'd chosen to set up shop in a control room in the most discreet part of the underground infrastructure. I'd spent many hours walking the metro before finally settling on a small powered room buried deep within the chute. If they found it, we were done for.

Michal placed the wrapped lab items on a table. His fingers shook when he looked back at me. "The … then what are they doing down there?"

I shrugged. "How should I know? Maybe they've taken to riding the subway to hell."

"Not amusing."

"Tell me about it." I shook my head and gave him a reassuring smile. "Listen, if I'm not back before a quarter till sunset, leave the stuff here and go back to the lab."

He nodded. "Okay. Just try and be quick and safe."

"Story of the new life, huh?"

I ignored the fear in his eyes and left him alone in the deserted warehouse. Despite the protection offered to the human citizens of Bloodfaye, we both knew District H was rife with dangers come nightfall. He would be a sitting duck. I wouldn't let him get plucked by some fangsta mongrel blood.

Adrenaline burned like fire as I descended the subway and emerged into the dark passageways. The air felt dank and cold against my skin, and a high-pitched scream chilled my bones. My breath was static and my boots light on grotty tiles as I moved forward. Putrid walls arched over me. *Flesh.* It was fresh and distinct, and it carried on the gust from the platform below. I stood at the top of the stairs and peered into the shadows. Laughter erupted. Everything was on high alert as I began taking the stairs and tried not to think about the danger I had forced upon my lifelong friend.

It was I who had collected the wolf-hybrid blood with plans to re-establish researching a cure for the Vampiric virus. And despite the supernatural blood running in my veins, it was I who breathed for nothing but the eradication of vampires from this world. The survival of humanity was stake enough. None so much as Michal's life. If he didn't survive, I'd never forgive myself.

3

HORROR IN THE SUBWAY

"*P*... please! No more!"

I stiffened. The woman's plea was met with laughter. My ears pricked and my blood stirred. The promise of violence called me as my veins yearned for blood. It was instinctual. I bit back and halted midway along the staircase, gripping the steel balustrade before taking a deliberate breath. The shadows seeped into my lungs like a felony. Footsteps echoed from the platform below. I focused on her breath. It was warm, erratic and sharp, and it was combined with another. Two humans. A hiss borrowed from a snake's vocal repertoire. *Silence.* An insinuating voice followed.

"But my dear, are you not having fun today?"

Zaros. The sound of him made me want to pull out his heart. My thoughts whirled. I knew the best thing to do was to return to Michal and wait for the cadaverous dimwits to complete their heinous amusement. Revealing my presence would be a daft move and may warrant unwanted curiosity. We did not need that. I went to turn around, but I stopped dead when I heard a horrendous growl and tearing flesh.

Shit. I palmed my dark hair. The woman gave a blood curdling scream and my brain began to split. I was no superhero. I had enough to deal with what with weird dreams, a vial of certain blood and Avila's disturbing relationship with overlord arrogance. A conversation intruded my inner world.

"Argh … easy, vampire! I wish to have my pleasure with her."

A snarling voice responded. "Take her, then."

The woman whimpered and yelped.

"The hawker skank has little pleasure to offer. She's already been used up good by the looks of her."

Chortles ensued but I barely heard them. No other thought materialized after that. I was pure focus. I started to move down the stairs toward the platform. *Damn.* Kindred or human, some things never changed – the best thing to do was not always the best thing to do.

A heavy thud sounded as I took the final step onto the subway platform. *Body dump.* I knew the sound well. Fluorescent tubes flickered sporadically along the upper ridges of the tunnel walls. The stale shaft air carried the stench of urine, sludge and blood. I scanned the stretch of tiled concrete edging along tracks that disappeared into a black abyss ahead. A strangled scream and more laughter. I collected my thoughts and dashed forward.

Liquidation. It aroused my senses as I stopped near a pillar and leaned against the worn poster that plastered chipped tiles. Zaros pinned a Leaving man against a wall and toyed with him. The man's face was shredded and bloody. Bits of flesh hung from beneath his eyes and his legs buckled as Zaros etched another vicious pattern across his brow. He laughed as his victim gave a distorted wail.

Loathing was vile in my gut. I stared at the three vampires standing over the woman slumped at their feet. Her blood flowed freely. Her body was slack. Black leather gleamed under the volatile lights. Kindred eyes shone like death as one of them gave her a few kicks with his boots.

The jackass voiced his thoughts. "She's fucking dead, stupid." His dark eyes blazed below straw-colored hair. He kicked the woman again. "So much for our afternoon entertainment."

A lofty creature with emeralds for eyes chuckled. His lips were swollen cherries. "She's still warm enough for you to get it on with her, stud."

"Do I look like Ricky? I'm not into necrophilia."

"Who are you kidding? I saw you giving it to that sweet little blondie vamp the other night – you think that's not necrophilia?"

"She was breathing, dipshit."

"Yeah, a breathing corpse."

They broke into laughter just as the man gave an agonizing scream. My eyes darted to Zaros as he growled and dug his fangs into his throat. The man's head lolled back and the sound of his fading pulse caught my ears as Zaros siphoned his blood. He would be dead in a matter of seconds.

To live or to die?

I did not wait to ponder the question any further. I pushed off the pillar to interrupt the sickening scene. In a flash of a movement, I was breathing down Zaros' neck. His odor was a mix of pungent blood and fleshy delight. "Release the Leaving, Zaros."

Surprise.

His jerky movement was executed gracefully. It was remarkable. He tore his fangs from the man's throat and snapped around to look at me. His talons sunk into the Leaving's shoulder and his black eyes beaded. Blood stuck on his twisting lips and clung to his chin. The others slinked up behind me as Zaros roared and flung the man across the platform. He landed like a ragdoll.

I grinned but it was tight. "Rather dramatic welcoming."

His black leathered shoulders curled forward, and he rolled his head. He let out a deep growl. His breath was right in my face and offensive, but that was the last thing on my mind. He was a tall and solid negro vampire with a hot temper. I packed a pretty decent build for a white-collared academic, but he was a force I could not ignore.

My grin dissolved and I steeled myself. I quickly sized up the situation – two goons behind and to my right and one on my left. I kept Zaros in sight. He hissed between bloodied lips and fangs. My temples throbbed but I did not flinch.

"What the fuck are you doing in the subway, *master J*? Shouldn't you be busy solving the meaning of life?"

The goons cracked up. I ignored them.

"Clearly you're busy destroying it."

"What?" He wiped blood from his chin before gesturing toward the Leavings. "You mean these scuzbucket hawker Leavings? Their lives are worthless."

"Marius would disagree. Bloodfaye was created as a haven for all Leavings with principles based on mutual faith. They agree to participate in the bloodletting cycle in exchange for protection from outside threats."

I paused and flicked my chin toward the man. He was still but moaned slightly. "This treatment is not in the interest of conserving our blood supply."

Zaros gave a cold laugh.

"Marius isn't the only vampire to overlord the city. If I wish to explore the occasional indulgence, I will do so at my own discretion." He moved closer and I stood my ground. "You may have won Marius' trust by returning to the city a victorious baby-wolf killer, but you don't fool me, Dr. Weird."

His crew edged up behind me.

"Trust is overrated in the new world." I glanced at the vampires who now leered with menace on all sides. "You may want to consider calling off the lost boys."

"Why would I do a silly thing like that?"

I gave a half laugh. "Because it is vital that an overlord possess the characteristics of a wise leader if he is to succeed in his quest to influence his clan."

He skimmed a bejeweled hand over his afro. "Like what?"

My lord, where do we begin?

"Like self-control and visions." I shrugged "Learning agility amid a changing landscape."

"You're suggesting I lack these qualities?"

I knew I was on dangerous ground but … I could not resist. "I'm suggesting you become more aware of these qualities."

He sucked in a breath and lunged at me. His fist slammed into my jaw and I stumbled against one of his cronies who promptly gripped my hair and yanked my head back.

Zaros' grisly image filled my vision. "You are one pretentious prick, lab rat." Razor talons seized my jaw. "I possess leadership qualities worse than any nightmare you've ever known."

Arrogance overload.

The one gripping my hair clenched his knuckles

tighter. My pulse exploded with venom. "I don't doubt that … but violence is not always the way to go."

The lost boys laughed. Zaros growled, his fangs dripping with saliva as he closed in on me. I flinched and swallowed, bracing myself. A sharp jab stabbed my side. I flinched but impact was minimal. I thrust back my elbow, digging into the inflexible ribs behind me. He jerked back enough for me to get free. I spun around with fangs bared.

The damned on the damned.

Stony eyes gleamed at me and the lofty vampire flicked his hair. "He is unappreciative. I want to see your nightmare leadership qualities, master."

Zaros grinned like a demonic idiot. "Right on."

He began to prowl forward. *Fuck.* My eyes flitted between them. Four to one. The odds were clearly against me. Adrenaline rushed. Zaros crouched for a strike. The others mimicked their master. A fire burst in my mind. I was ready.

A shrill voice reverberated through the tunnel and stung my ears.

"Zaros, stop!"

I glanced beyond the vamps as Sun strode across the platform. Her eyes narrowed but she was a pleasant vision. Her leather boots clanked noisily as her breasts protruded beneath white fabric. She looked pissed.

Zaros and his gang whirled to look at her. Sassy female vampire. She had come into her own. Her lips crimped as her gaze trailed to me before noting the Leavings on the platform beyond me. "What's going on down here?"

Zaros was all cheese. His fangs almost blinded me as he squared his shoulders. "Sun, always a pleasure to see you."

"Master Zaros." She gave him a cool stare and moistened her lips. "District H curfew is almost upon us. Marius has half of the city out searching for you."

"Is that so?"

"Yes."

He regarded her silently. A moment passed. "This scene was getting old anyways. We're done here for now."

Sun nodded and he moved closer to her. "I will be seeing *you* later."

She did not reply as he motioned for his crew and strode from the platform without looking back at me. The exchange perked my interest, but it fast faded when emerald eyes moved in front of me and hissed in my face. *Buffoon.* My upper lip lifted as he spun around and followed the others.

Sun came up beside me. "You okay?"

"Yeah. Thanks. Michal filled you in?"

"He was concerned." She gestured toward the Leavings. "One still lives."

"He won't make it."

Her eyes glowed like honey "He needs to; he's perfect. You're going to need him."

"Huh? Why?"

"Obviously he hasn't been processed into the district, yet."

"And?"

"For a smart guy, you can be awfully dumb, Jett. You will eventually need a loyal vampire to complete your experiment. Who better than a sired?"

My mouth fell open. "You want me to sire him?"

"Yes." Her voice was gentle and she reached for my hand. "Come on."

I said nothing more and allowed her to guide me. *The best thing to do is not always the best thing to do.* But who ever really knew what that was? A million thoughts erupted. None could comprehend the woman next to me. She was half angel, half minx, and she was a thief of the expected.

DEATH IS COMING

"Am I alive?"

"You're not dead."

"I'm not alive either."

I looked toward the sea. The water glistened like gothic black and the air was motionless. *Am I breathing?* I knew nothing in that moment and yet I felt a strange sense of tranquility. It was her presence. *Melissa.* The tips of her fingers found my nape and her voice was melodic.

"There are no accidents, Jett."

She smiled. I missed her smile.

"You're dead," I said. Her touch felt like a remedy. "We're both dead."

Coffee-colored eyes grew turbulent as she looked beyond me. Her lips thinned. A crow's call rang out across the shoreline followed by a hideous laugh. My skin crawled. The atrocious sound was familiar. Avila's shriek was the next thing I heard as I spun around to face a pair of beaded eyes on weathered skin. I sucked in a breath. I *was* breathing.

Ginger-beard – the hawker responsible for Scarla's death and the darkness that had claimed my daughter. I had ripped his ugly head from his neck some time ago and yet here he stood with his skull intact and his filthy arms ensnaring Avila. His scruffy boots dug into the sand. Crows hovered above him like a bad omen as he grinned with grisly intent. "I'm taking her with me to hell, blood-hustler!"

Avila appeared stoic as the earth parted beneath them and they began to sink into the grainy terrain. *Landslide.* Horror was an affliction. My lungs burned and I went to move but stopped short when Melissa's fingers clawed my arm. I barely heard her speak over my pounding heart.

"There are no accidents, Jett. My death … your death."

"Huh?" I frowned and twisted my arm from her grasp as Ginger-beard laughed before he began whistling a raspy tune.

The Doors: *This is the End.*

"This is the end, beautiful friend."

His barbed tone stung my psyche. I roared and bolted toward their submerging figures, lunging for Avila just as the sand edged beneath her chin. She peered at me silently and her eyes began to pool with blood as I desperately burrowed into the sand threatening to swallow her entirely. The suction was relentless. She sunk deeper into the cool sand without so much as a whimper. Ginger-beard paused his song to cackle some more as the beach devoured him like a noiseless vacuum.

My throat constricted. "No!"

The crows cawed louder above the rhythmic sound of the waves colliding against the seashore. The salty air caved in around me. Blood tears blistered across my daughter's pale face as I worked franticly to scoop the sand away from her. It was useless – I couldn't stop the incessant force.

"Avila!" I grasped at her dark hair as her face disappeared. *Fuck!* My grip tightened around strands of the black silk slipping through my fingers as the beach ingested her whole.

"A ... Avila!"

A stupefied moment. The distinct sound of a black wing. A haunting voice of the long dead.

"No accidents, Jett."

A wicked laugh and Ginger-beard spluttered as the beach closed in around his throat. His dark eyes gleamed and he crooned. "I'll never look into your eyes again."

"Motherfucker!" I cried.

I growled and repeatedly slammed my fist into his face. The sound of his crunching bones did nothing to satisfy the madness. Blood like artwork over gleaming sand. I knew nothing. *Nothing.* The sandy grains fell into his gaping mouth and he gurgled as I smashed his head further into the earth. Then he was gone and so was my baby girl. I remained, trembling.

There was a gentle touch on my shoulder. Melissa. Her sound was unwelcome as I began to extract myself from the disturbing nightmare.

"She has a secret, Jett."

"She's gone."

"Death is coming."

I forced my eyes open and focused on the ceiling. My head felt somewhat clammy and my fingers tingled. Night terrors. Who would have thought the undead could dream? If you could call it that. Melissa was coming to me more often and the messages were growing in intensity. Vampires can't dream the dreams of the spirited. We were denied such pleasures. We didn't deserve them.

I studied my palms and noticed they appeared to shimmer in the dark. I looked like the flipside of a dark star. I shimmied in black. A moonlit forest drenched in rain. *Interesting.* This is what sweat looked like to a vampire. It was one of our more appealing characteristics that I found fascinating. I sweat chocolate twinkies but I'm no delight.

I stretched out over my bed. Yes, I owned a bed and a

big-ass brownstone on a quaint little street in District V. We even had trees lining the curbs – big green maples with luscious leaves that gathered above the street like a canopy. It added a slice of normalcy in a completely abnormal world. It wasn't always such a bad thing to try to forget every now and then. Not that Melissa was letting me do much of that lately.

Death is coming.

I think she was off a good two years on that score. I gave a half laugh and rose from my bed. Death had long ago arrived in the form of biological warfare experiments gone wrong which resulted in the incurable V-virus but I knew the woman meant to deliver an ominous message. Something was up. I couldn't remember the last time I'd dreamed of her – five, maybe seven years? Whatever the time, she had now managed to forge a real connection to my dream world and I wasn't digging it.

"Melissa, Melissa – can't you just be a little clearer about your messages?"

It was like trying to solve a cryptic puzzle and with everything else going on – prepping to begin viral cultures with the hybrid blood while at the same time upholding the 'good vampire citizen' image, as well as dealing with egotistical overlords and trying to keep incoming Leavings alive – I didn't possess enough time or energy to decipher her riddles.

I padded into the bathroom to douse myself with cold water, pausing to peer at my reflection. My eyes appeared as icy as the water below my thick brows and my ageless features were strange to me. Vampires were simulated creatures. There was nothing real in the unfamiliar sight staring back at me. Nothing but unearthly death and the remnants of a scrupulous heart.

It was hanging on by a thread.

Ha. What would Clio say about my "pure heart" planning to overthrow the kindred? Clio was the witch who helped to cover up the truth about the wolf-baby, Shana. The first generation of Blood Legend who Marius believed I had killed. As far as I knew, Clio remained hidden in the mountains with Shana and her mother. She had been adamant that we must wait for the hybrid blood to mature through the generations before vampires could be eradicated, but patience was never my strongest suit. I wanted them gone now. I wanted to be human again.

Would Clio think I was on a death wish? I frowned at the mirror. Why did I even care what the witch would think?

Hmm...

I'd be lying if I said my thoughts didn't often dwell on her, Sienna and Shana, but I wasn't about to mention those names out loud in the blood city. It was tedious enough that I had Shana's secrets tucked away in a vial of her blood, much less speak of my deception to the clan. Avila didn't even know. It's not that I didn't trust her, it was just too risky considering her connection with Marius.

The wolf-mother and her Blood Legend baby still breathed, but I sure as hell wouldn't be if that little piece of intel spilled into the wrong ears. That's why I wished to keep digging to cure the V-virus – to further protect what was left of Scarla's family and my own. Besides, imagine all the human lives spared in a world without bloodsuckers.

Action was required. I tried to shrug off the ghastly images of Avila's dream-death but I couldn't stop the sense of urgency rippling through me. If I could still pee, I'd be pissing a fountain right now. As it was, my innards were a dried-up wasteland that absorbed blood like a rapacious sponge. There were never any leftovers to warrant a good piss. Nostalgia was fleeting as I glanced at the toilet. I think I missed pissing as much as eating real food.

Get a grip, Jett. Pissing and food paled in comparison to the prospect of Avila's death. Michal and I had to get to work on the hybrid blood promptly. We had gathered enough supplies to start and now we even had a test-dummy in the form of Draven, the subway kid I'd regenerated, to test the experimental vaccines. He was currently holed up with Sun and I was eager to get to him. I had sired him and knew making a firm connection was necessary in gaining his trust if we were to use him in our little covert venture.

Ah, the things we must do to invoke change.

The faint sounds of Avila tramping around downstairs

drifted through the crack of my bedroom door as I pulled on a blazer. I didn't bother to gaze out of the window at the pre-dawn light. The dome always misconstrued the time of day anyway and I knew it was still early.

Nocturnal creatures attempting to sleep at night as if they were still human was somewhat amusing, but the dome made it possible and it worked well for managing the Leavings. They were our lifeforce. It had been an adjustment, but my body clock was finally catching up to the new routine.

As I made for the stairs, I toyed with the idea of slipping from the house undetected. Things were proving a tad dicey on the home front of late. It was my fault. I called it realism, but I knew that I wasn't making it easy for Avila by withholding my approval of her relationship with Marius. She called it pigheaded genes.

I hit the bottom of the stairs and stopped briefly near an antique mahogany side table in the tiled entrance hall. Although not overly large, the high ceilings gave the area an open vibe. I looked up toward the delicate crystal chandelier overhead and listened. Avila loved that elaborate fixture but it did nothing for me. I kept it for her.

All was quiet. I detected no movement coming from the other parts of the house but for the monotonous ticking of the stately grandfather clock in the sitting room. I strode toward the door, freezing like the guilty when her voice sounded behind me.

"Dad?"

"Yup?" I spun on my heels with a sheepish grin that fast dissolved when I saw her face. She leaned against the wall in a pair of white pajamas, twisting the ends of her long dark hair. Her azure eyes flashed. I frowned. "Are you okay?"

She gave an abrupt sob before rushing to me. I pulled her in tightly as she buried her chin against my chest and cried. It was a sight I hadn't witnessed for the longest of times.

"What is it, Avila?"

"It … it's mom."

5

WHIP-HAPPY

It was late afternoon when I marched along the District H streets after spending the day working the laboratory. Sun was going to take me back to her place so that I could meet the kid from the subway. It was important that I establish a bond with my sired.

I knew it instinctively. I was also instinctively acquainted with the ache in my shoulders from hours hunched over benchtops and processing dozens of Leavings through District H. It was times like these that I was grateful for my rejuvenation gifts.

I couldn't say the same about my current surroundings. The stale air was a pungent combo of food waste and human excrement. I kept my mouth shut and my eye on the endgame. I had agreed with Michal that something had to be done about the living conditions here.

Perhaps I could figure out a way to improve the situation if I pushed past my deep resistance to converse with Marius. *Who knew how long it could take for us to cultivate a working cure? – Months? Years?* Our Leavings deserved to exist in some version of dignity in the meantime.

Marius. My hackles rose at the thought of him. It was the hold he had on Avila. She inexplicably adored him. I cracked my knuckles and increased my pace. I had to believe that whatever was going on between them would run its course. After all, I had raised her to use her smarts when it came to the opposite sex.

I had to trust that intuitive instincts would prevail. The alternative was not up for contemplation when there was a kindred-less future to think about.

I took the final corner to the street that would take me back into vampire territory. Also known as District V. The usual hustle near the iron-meshed gates that intersected along the great wall was in full swing.

The gates were heavily guarded around the clock and provided the sole pathway between the districts. It was a popular area since the implementation of the slavery program because those gates transitioned us between worlds – vampire masters and their human slaves.

The fictitious cliché involving humans serving vampires had outsmarted reality. Generation V had arrived to revolutionize real-world beliefs and it was a riot of the irony. Nevertheless, Leavings were strictly prohibited to wander District V without the accompaniment of their master.

It was one of our most scrupulous rules that gave me no end of amusement. Show me a Leaving stupid enough to venture a vampire-infested district alone and I'll show you a chicken with lips.

The smirk was wiped from my face when I heard a series of hollering ahead as four cackling Mysticus guards came into view. They stood in front of the Norbury City Library jeering at the group of Leavings scouring the hundreds of books that lay scattered and torn among broken desks, chairs, and lamps at the building's entrance. My approach went unnoticed, and I stopped behind the guards to assess the scene.

About ten Leavings were loading the debris into a large dumpster while two others stood at the library threshold heaving furniture through the doors and chucking books onto the mounting pile.

The entire staircase leading toward the library entrance was a chaotic wreckage. Even though I was aware of Marius' plans to gut the building to make way for a communal food hall for the Leavings, witnessing our literature discarded in such a flippant manner was deeply disturbing. More alarming was that the task at hand appeared to have discharged the mounting frustration in the Leavings.

They roamed, picked, and tore through the disarray in

their ragged clothes and spilt boots, and they were all making a ruckus. I could sense their brusque disdain in the stuffy air as one crazy guard cracked a whip against the sidewalk while he and his pals cheered on the vandals.

"Shred 'em good, shitbags!" The brawny guard sniggered. "That's right, fuck with ya history. You won't live long enough for it to matter, anyway."

The guards cackled before another waved a fist. "Come on, Leavings, show us what you've got – my bitches 'vag' gives more destruction than you lot!"

If this quartet had a brain between them, they'd be deadly dangerous. As it was, they were unpredictably risky. The vibe among the Leavings was beginning to border on rage, and it was sickening. I couldn't just walk on and leave these humans under the precarious watch of these vampires. Things took a dark turn when one Leaving man bent to his knees amid the carnage and raised a book above his head.

The tarnished lettering that embellished the worn leather caught my eye right away, while tears broke through the layer of grime on his face as he looked at the bible balancing overhead. His quivering voice was faint.

"This is for Christ our Savior who failed us." He released a wrangled sob before he began mauling the scripture like a madman. Torn pages hung askew as he cursed God.

The guards in front of me laughed and nudged each other.

"It's book week in downtown District Hell, dirtwads!" The whip-happy guard hissed and cracked the leathers. The scuffed straps split a timber chair like a buttersnap cookie and narrowly missed a Leaving woman. He laughed as the woman screeched and whirled around, spitting dirty orange hair from her face, and waving a splintered table leg. *If looks could kill.*

"Back off, leech. You almost did kill me!" Her nimble fingers gripped the fractured pale of wood aimed at his heart as he stepped closer to her. She gave a loud snort. "Just try it, clot-buster, and you'll find out what happens next."

Had she totally lost her mind?

In the next moment, the whip was on the gravel and the guard had the woman ensnared between his claws and her head pushed back with her throat fully exposed.

The splintered stake she held clanked to the ground. He gave a vicious hiss and grinned at his cronies as she screamed. The other three guards watched on, stupefied, while every Leaving stopped their pickings.

Surely this jackass guard knew better than to feed directly from a dome Leaving. One could only hope that he was savvy enough to avoid the harsh penalties involved in such a violation.

He would face countless weeks holed up in the roach-infested cells beneath the city with only stray rats for feed. But hope was lost on the undead soul whose heavy-lidded eyes beheld his captive. My nerves tingled as I contemplated the situation, watching as the vampire rolled back his neck and bared his fangs.

Time was up. I took off like the wind, charging toward him as he gnawed into the woman's throat. The fragrance of the woman's blood dominated my senses as I slammed my palm into the guard's forehead. Bone collision. I felt his skull fracture before his head recoiled with the brutal impact.

He snarled and stumbled backward, stomping heavily onto the debris underfoot. He leapt back to his feet and growled at me with his razor nails poised.

"Game over, blood-mongrel. Do you really want to dance with the devil today?" I said.

I stared him down as he considered his options, daring him to make the next move as the moment gave way to a whimper and a faint heartbeat. *Ba-boom. Ba-boom.* The vampire withdrew his claws to smear the back of a hand across his mouth. *Ba-boom. Ba-boom.* He smirked and began to slink away as the woman's eyes rolled up as she started to collapse. I caught her as the sound of Sun's voice called from behind.

"Jett! What the hell?"

I glanced around as she strutted forth clad in a white leather mini-dress and matching knee-high boots. Her platinum hair was piled atop her crown and the silver hoops adorning her lobes caught the afternoon glow offered by the dome canopy. She appeared angelic until she halted beside the guards and glared.

"Baboons! Treating Leavings in this way is completely unacceptable. Shame on all of you!"

They reacted with a shrug before seeking solace in the dirt at their feet. I lowered the woman and tore the fabric of my undershirt so that I could wrap her throat wound. A skittish Leaving man rushed to her side as she groaned. She would survive the vampire attack and I was thankful.

I adjusted my jacket sleeves and joined Sun. "Just an ordinary day in Bloodfaye city."

"Who the hell is in charge of this shit-show, anyway?"

"I am!"

Zaros. I groaned inwardly as his voice carried from the library threshold. "Surprise, surprise."

He grinned and started for the stairs as Sun gave him a death stare. He stopped short of us and regarded his crew before he glanced between Sun and me.

"What did I miss?"

"These vampires are mishandling our Leavings." I gestured toward the whip-happy guard. "That one attacked and fed from a Leaving woman."

Zaros' eyes flashed. "Thank you, master J. I'll take it from here and deal with them accordingly."

"Yes, right after Marius' announcement," Sun said. "He has summoned all Mysticus members for an audience in the Crypt courtyard at once."

"What for?"

"Nobody knows."

I ignored Zaros as he barked an order at his guards, instructing them to take the offender away. I frowned. "Charming. Another surprise, surprise."

6

MERCY

"How's the kid doing?"

"Fine. The kid has a name, you realize."

"You just saw our historical literature destroyed like yesterday's news. Names mean nothing now."

"Does to him." Sun glanced at me as we walked toward the Crypt. The streets were almost barren. "You should try to remember his name considering that he is to play host to your cure thingy."

"Thingy? That's one way of putting it."

"Forgive me if I'm not up to speed on clinical jargon."

I grinned. "Forgiven."

She did have a point. The kid from the subway was vital to me, but our prearranged meeting would have to wait. We were en route to hear Marius' big surprise announcement. The kid's name was the last thing on my mind as I scanned the District V streets. This side of the wall was the opposite to the slums that our Leavings were forced to endure. Everything was clean, shiny, and proper, and apart from a few strays, the usual freak-fair hive was lost on the bogus shopfronts and blood cafes. I liked it. Fake-faced vampire society had momentarily ceased, and the peaceful vibe somehow echoed my resolve behind forming the secret sector. A world where people didn't turn into blood-lust creatures was all I wanted for Avila and the rest of humanity.

Sun gestured toward the dome shell that blazed above us in an orange haze. "Always my favorite time of day – dusk."

"I know what you mean."

It was another reason to find the cure. I would give anything to again witness those breaking hours between night and day with my naked eye. I looked heavenward with longing. Dawn and dusk had always kept me grounded, reminding me what it meant to be alive. Now, I was nothing but a walking corpse who may never again know the revelation of a new day, much less the striking secrets of sunset. I didn't want to think about that prospect. Not when there was hope.

I jammed my hands in my pockets as the sound of the crowd gathering in the Crypt courtyard thrummed in my ears. *Busy bees swarming a honey jar.* We were about a block away from the laughter and chattering that carried along the treetops and brownstones. My stomach tightened. I was having trouble aligning with the fact that this was the first time Marius had summoned the entire clan on a whim to make an announcement. Obviously, something was up. Sun encroached my thoughts.

"Any idea about all this?"

"Nope." We rounded a corner, and the crowded Crypt courtyard came into view. "Maybe he's discovered a cure before me and wishes to free us from hell and damnation."

"Fat chance. You know how much he loves vampirism hell and damnation of new world order."

I did indeed. As did the few hundred vampires congregating in front of a timber stage that stood in the courtyard like an oiled oasis beneath an elaborate maze of wrought iron. I paused to take in the black iron twisting into glyphs and symbols that represented vampire folklore. A chill passed through me as my gaze settled on the brass candelabras wafting the scent of roses all around, pungently seductive above the four indigenous vampires who stood like stoic statues along the back of the stage, drums poised. The scene was dramatic, mystical, and deeply disturbing. It was all I could do as I looked at the dozens of fresh, scarlet flowers that gracefully entwined the iron.

"Some kind of set-up," I said.

Marius had transformed the Crypt courtyard into a public arena of sorts, but it wasn't the newly furbished courtyard that got under my skin as much as the underlying hint of romance in the air. *Smokescreens and deceit.* It was a biting stench that rose the hairs on my neck, reminding me why I avoided the Crypt as much as possible. The Crypt itself had been a place of worship in the old world. The lofty sandstone building was a majestic temple with a historical soul that Marius had claimed as his own. There was nothing holy about the place now. It reeked like stale blood and bullshit.

"Our overlord flirts with passion. He sure knows how to make a hellish impression for the nameless." Sun grinned before flicking her chin toward the fanged crowd. "Come on, let's crash the mosh pit."

"Don't you mean death pit?"

The death pit defied all universal laws in that it resembled a posse of waking dead extortionists overloaded with glitzy glares, florid lips, and an unmistakable sense of entitlement. All set firmly on pallid faces. I could have been amid the crazy bizarre on Bourbon Street during Mardi Gras. And I was one of the freaks.

Mercy.

I'd be lying if I said that a part of me was not dark, blood-hungry, and primitive. Even the purest of hearts is drawn to the allure of darkness. The urge to succumb to my preternatural instincts was my greatest pleasure and adversary. I was a walking contradiction battling my demons at the best of times. It's amazing what deep hatred could do to a man. It was almost as strong as love.

I followed Sun through the strange throng, making our way closer to the stage. A thousand snippets of disembodied voices trailed me.

"Oh, this is so exciting! I just love surprises!"

Ha. That makes one of us.

"Where is Marius? Do you see him?"

"No but check out the—"

Black locks flicked in my face as I passed.

"Heaven on earth, maybe we're going to get a taste of new blood!"

"That ain't gonna happen in the blood dome, baby."

A drawn-out hiss was swallowed by the crowd behind me.

"Who're ya calling baby, anal-ant?"

I weaved my way forward. Marius was encouraging an aristocratic lifestyle in District V. Some of us embraced it, others still secretly longed to feed as their kindred nature intended. But none of that mattered in this moment as every conversation gave way to a collective gasp followed by the smooth tempo of drums. I stopped dead in my tracks as Marius strode onto the stage suited up in white leather and gold and sporting a huge grin alongside Avila.

Huh?

The mob applauded and cheered all around me while I scratched my chin in the stupid hope the action might unclog my thoughts as I watched my daughter on stage. She appeared to glide along the timber boards in the full-length black dress that swept in her wake as she clutched Marius' hand, stopping front center on the stage. Her usually milky-white cheeks flushed and her eyes flared violet in the candlelight, contrasting against her dark hair. The beating drums subsided, and the crowd hushed.

I had never seen that dress nor had I seen her look so happy since before the apocalypse shredded our lives to madness. *What the hell is going on here?* I couldn't quite piece together the unfolding events, nor could I stop the wrenching in my gut when Marius combed a hand through his jet locks and laughed before addressing the audience.

"Dear Mysticus vampires, it pleases me to see you here. Thank you for allowing me to intrude upon your dusk hour, and with little warning no less. Your presence is much cherished."

Cherished? What a schmuck.

The crowd broke into the expected round of applause while Marius swept his arms in a grandeur fashion, gracefully receiving their reverence. Always the artful snake in the grass. He may have the majority fooled, but my knuckles ached as much the sly look on his face and I longed to rearrange those perfectly chiseled features. I focused back on Avila as Marius shushed the crowd before continuing to charm and seduce by offering a velvety slab of verbal vomit.

He gestured around the stage. "I can sense your

growing curiosity. I bet you are wondering what this lovely optic spitball is all about, hmm?"

"Yes! Tell us!"

"It's the new Vampire's Ball!"

"Marius, I adore you!"

An eruption of laughter.

"I adore you too, my lovely! I adore all of you!" Marius pointed at the crowd. "Welcome to the new Vampire's Ball!"

The pack cheered, clapped and cooed at our lordship while my kid remained silent. I wanted to rush up there and collect her. I wanted to take her some place far away from these poisonous people and stop the darkness from consuming her world, but I couldn't move as Marius waited for the crowd to quieten before finally getting to the point of it all.

"Of course, I'm only half-kidding about the Vampire's Ball."

He reached for Avila's hand before he looked at the audience. Sun glanced at me and frowned, and my boots anchored deeper into the lawn as I watched my daughter.

"I've said it before and I'll say it again – the path toward ascension for the Mysticus clan is undoubtedly paved with alignment, awakening and union. We do have cause for much celebration. As your overlord, I have kept my word and provided you the freedom to safely enjoy daylight hours once again. I have equipped you with an endless supply of blood in our Bloodfaye Leavings. You all dwell in comfortable homes with all the pleasures of the old world – I think suffice it to say that I have given you a quality of life that you never would have found outside of the dome."

He paused as the crowd applauded, then his voice rose over the cheering. "I give you all of these comforts away from outside threats. Now, it is time to initiate the next component in the quest for us to become the world's most powerful clan – union."

Marius glanced at Avila before he raised her hand in the air. "When next month's full moon appears in five weeks' time, I will claim my divine feminine as my own in the first Mysticus Claiming Ceremony! The two of us will merge our supernatural gifts into one loving dynamic as we revolutionize the world toward ascension. Ladies and gentlemen, I give you the future Vampire Queen – Lady Avila!"

Lady what?

The crowd exploded into a joyous roar and Sun looked at me. Her pale face was a vague impression as my world shattered.

7

ACRIMONY

The beating drums became a distinct timbre of grief. My hands shook uncontrollably. *My girl!* I swallowed my pain along with the goblets of blood on offer as the crowd moved as if in a trance. The courtyard had fast transformed into a primitive dance of passion and erotica. Hips grinded and swayed. Euphoric moaning morphed into hissing and biting. This is what celebration looked like to the kindred. Their glossy hair gleamed beneath the inky dome shell as they groped, danced, and clawed while I stood frozen amid the psychedelic orgy. Each moment was like death as I faced the prospect of losing my little girl all over again.

Sun grabbed my arm. Her voice seemed distant. "Jett?"

I stared ahead. "She didn't tell me."

A Claiming Ceremony? I peered past the freakshow

toward the stage in time to see Marius and Avila slip between the side curtains. *Impossible.* There was no way that Avila could become the Vampire Queen. Not my kid. It was obvious that such a stature carried dire consequences. A Vampire Queen of a powerful clan would make a primary target for every mongrel blood with half a backbone. And even more disturbing was that I feared the powerful position would rob her of what was left of her humanity. She would mirror her king and turn off her "humanity" switch. That was unacceptable. Marius must be influencing her. He *was* the one who had sired her. I felt a thunderous rush of rage hit me.

"I'm sorry," Sun said.

"About what?"

"That she didn't—"

The rest of her words were a mystery as I raced through the twilight weird-fest fueled by the rage within me. I broke from the crowd and paused at the edge of the courtyard. My nocturnal vision kicked in as I peered around and homed in on his smug masculine scent. Sunset was over and the dusky glow blazing across the dome had long sunk into night. I planted my feet wide, scanning the stretch of manicured lawns, cobbled pathways, and rows of rose bushes that studded the Crypt grounds before my sights settled on the Crypt itself. The domed cathedral appeared elegantly opaque with its leadlight windows and angelic statues but I saw none of it as I tuned out the celebratory background noise and into the muffled laughter drifting from around the back of the stage.

Marius and Avila. Their intimate conversation was daggers to my mind and fueled the dark energy within. Destruction beckoned. It was as gritty as dirt and it smothered my chest to reveal the agonizing truth: I was a vampire. *I am death.*

The emotions ruled me, and clarity was an illusion. Each moment I spent resisting my instincts to kill was nullified. I was the nameless creature of nightmares with a bloodthirsty heart. The compulsion for violence surged through me and I almost wanted to explode. Everything is nothing without her. She was all I had left in the post V-virus world. I bolted toward the sound of their conversation as my feet scorched the earth. I was going to shred Marius alive.

I found him leaning against the trunk of a tree with Avila in his arms. He was caressing her hips and speaking in a lover's tongue as she leaned in close and teased him. *Voodoo-born mind games.* Vampires exceled at trickery and seduction. They were among our greatest assets. Avila knew it. I lingered in the shadows near the backstage framework as I surveyed the area. A few guards were watching the outer grounds but none were in our immediate location. My shoulders were back in fine form as I snarled and prowled forward.

Avila gasped and spun around to face me. "Dad?"

I splayed my fingers and approached while two

guards appeared like magic from the shadows. They were skulking the lawn like ancient warmongers, and stunk like day-old semen. Their white leather glimmered in my peripheral vision as Marius lifted a palm to stop them. They made no noise when they slid back into the shadows a few feet away while Marius stared back at me. *Insentient.* His eyes were a fossilized relic as I closed in before Avila stepped between us.

"Dad, stop!"

She gripped my arms and I halted abruptly. My vision blurred as her eyes became dewy and I tried to focus on her. "I should have told you, I'm sorry."

Her touch was almost anecdotal.

"Told me what exactly?"

"About our plans for the Claiming Ceremony. I should have given you a heads up."

"Heads up? Interesting choice of words, Avila."

"How so?"

"My *head* is throbbing mad because I just discovered that the only thing getting up and into your head of late is an alarming case of vampire brainwashing! No thanks to your overlord here." I glared at Marius. It was all I could do to tame my seething appetite. "You are *not* going to be the Vampire Queen."

Her jaw dropped and Marius sniggered behind her.

"Get a grip, Dad. This is *my* life and *my* decision, not yours. Do I have to remind you that Marius is your overlord too?" She gave a nervous laugh. "I know you are upset, but you're looking at this in the wrong way. No one here is your enemy. I am sorry that I didn't tell you, but I knew how you'd react."

"And how's that, Avila?"

"Like a hot-headed, stuffy-ass control freak. Must we do this here?"

"You didn't leave me much choice."

"No, I was the one left with little choice because of your fixed mindset about the new world."

What? Fixed mindset? Ludicrous.

I was about to respond when the definition of fixed mindset spoke up.

"She's right, Jett." Marius pushed off the trunk and approached. "We're all in this together. The new world, the Mysticus, and creating a new way of being. The transition has been difficult but I can now see the light at the end of the tunnel. Can you not see how this union is exactly what the clan needs to bring a sense of hope for the future?"

"Hope for the future? The future is as deceptive as the sky overhead. Nobody can foresee a favorable future in a virus-riddled world. You will bring her misery and death. It is too dangerous. I forbid it."

"Forbid it? Unbelievable! Dad, I can—"

Marius drowned her voice when he laughed.

"Come now, no need to be so dramatic. We've come a long way already in this virus-riddled world, as you so eloquently put it." He gestured around him. "Open your eyes, Jett. I have flipped a chaotic city on its head to create a controlled and safe environment for vampires and humans to coexist. Avila is safe with me. Surely the noble principles behind Bloodfaye satisfies your urban warrior heart?"

"Are you kidding me?"

I stepped into his personal space. The guards were breathing down my neck in an instant as my words minced on old hate.

"You dare to mock my *urban warrior heart* after stealing my daughter's humanity and then persuading her to agree to this bullshit ceremony business?"

I barely felt Avila pull at my arm as she said my name. Marius responded with a tight grin. His face was like an ambiguous mask before he glanced between the guards and waved them away. They retreated slightly as Marius licked his lips and leaned in close.

"Let us not forget that I have been gracious enough to allow you to live after you betrayed my trust and discarded the only known vial of AB positive blood known to exist."

He reached for Avila's hand and I tried to control my vampiric cravings as he continued. "Whether you give us your consent or not, I *am* going to take your daughter as the first Mysticus Vampire Queen because it is what she wants of me. Obviously, we would prefer to have your support in our shared vision to achieve ascension as the most powerful clan in the world ...." His voice trailed and he shrugged. "If you cannot bring yourself to the table, for Avila's sake, I will continue to allow you to live in your own misery so long as you obey Mysticus rules. Do we understand each other?"

Incineration.

I went to tell him that he could shove his rules right up his pompous backside when I looked at Avila. She gnawed her bottom lip and her eyes appeared like sea-glass gems pleading with me. I squeezed my eyes shut and collected the rage at the tip of my tongue, taking a deliberate breath before looking back at her.

"This is what you want?"

"With all my heart."

Her reply was enough to finish what was left of my urban warrior heart. I was losing her to a power-hungry slavedriver and there was nothing I could do to stop it. All at once, Marius' sordid words fell at my feet and I saw the baby girl who I had adored and protected since birth. I had set this wheel in motion the day I had left her with Marius in favor of saving humanity.

It was reliving my failure all over again.

8

I WANT TO SHOW YOU SOMETHING

"I can barely remember her. I mean, I know what she looks like but it's hard to recall the way she was as a woman and a mother."

Avila stopped and looked up. One half of the dome was illuminated like rustic gold with the rising sun but that wasn't her focus. I followed her gaze to see a handful of sparrows in flight.

She frowned. "Birds?"

I grinned. "They've found a way in."

She laughed. "I like it."

"Me too."

She fell quiet as we walked the sleepy District V streets. This section of the dome was a far cry from the crud on the other side of the wall. Marius was sprucing up the place. Everything from shopfronts and buildings to every brownstone on every block. He was committed to ensuring a high living standard for the Mysticus clan and took great measures to create a sense of belonging and purpose for us. Naturally, they celebrated his generosity. There was nothing selfless about his benevolence, though. That much I knew.

The fact was currency was no longer an issue in the new world where the kindred reigned supreme. Now, all things were available to us on a whim. Most Mysticus members had never lived a better life before this one. Marius knew it. They were easy to appease. It will be interesting to see what happens when familiarity sets in. *Contempt.* They'll be expecting a mile soon enough.

"What was she really like, dad?"

"She was … like you; beautiful inside and out." We paused on the sidewalk at a crossroad. Golf carts were parked along the curb on the street ahead. Marius was slowly introducing a means of transport to the citizens of District V. I had to admit that it was a great perk. Vampires were a snobby bunch at heart. We'd rather catch a ride than to waste precious supernatural energy where possible. It made us feel civilized. I wanted one.

Avila watched me. "Why did you love her?"

The streets ahead were livening up. It was the main thoroughfare. I gestured toward the opposite direction where the avenues remained subdued. Inner-city vampire suburbia resembled the old world beneath a sleek sky canopy. We could almost pretend to be human that way. It was ironic.

"This way," I said.

She fell into step beside me as we took a corner to a street that led nowhere. I took a moment to relish the first real conversation I'd managed with Avila since my emotional outburst over Marius' big announcement. "Why does anyone love anyone?"

She stuffed her hands in her pockets. Her nose scrunched. "What do you mean?"

I shrugged. "There were billions of people on earth before the virus struck, Avila, and most of them loved someone. Yet, no one who has ever fully abandoned themselves to deep love can ever articulate the experience enough to justify the feelings."

"Sounds intense."

"Love is intense." I pulled her close, squeezing an arm around her shoulder like I did when she was a little girl. "I love *you* intense."

"Hmm … that's a different kind of love. You're my father."

"Doesn't make it any less significant. There are all kinds of love – not everyone is capable of giving and receiving deep love, least of all the kindred."

Her eyes flickered up at me. "You haven't answered my question."

"Oh, you think I'm deflecting?" I smiled and nodded toward a tall vampire dressed in a beetroot-red suit as he passed. It was frightful attire, but I was growing accustomed to the odd sense of fashion favored by the kindred. Personally, I preferred a more reserved look. I now owned an impressive collection of suits. Most of them were black. "Let me see … I loved your mother for her unusual quirks and quiet habits. Her passion for biomedical genetics and cracking genetic codes was admirable. She loved her work, though she was unable to share most of what snared her attention away from us due to company privacy policies. It was extremely alluring nonetheless."

"Ha!" She nudged her shoulder into me. Her voice was feathery. "Only a scientist nerd would consider genetic code-cracking attractive."

"You've got that right – but only those who love bloodwork and DNA analysis could actually understand what I mean." I laughed. "Which, of course, is now just about the majority of the population."

Avila snorted. "Not so much. We just love to ingest blood by default. Not study the stuff."

"Well, I loved your mom by default. Couldn't help myself. She kept a secret smile just for me and no one else. I loved that about her. She had a knack for driving me crazy too, but I loved every moment of our life together."

She gave a soft laugh. "She used to play music."

"Hip Hop was her weakness. Go figure."

Avila stiffened and pulled away. "I miss her, dad. More than ever; as if we've just lost her."

"We never stop missing someone we have loved."

She groaned. "Why do you always have to be so philosophical about everything?"

The question had some interest, but she wasn't looking for a reply. She followed up rather quickly.

"It gets old … fast."

"Well, I'm just …"

"I don't need your philosophy to know that I am getting married soon and she isn't here to share it with me." Her arms flailed. "No one is around to tell me how to love a man or how to be a wife or help me choose the right dress while we laugh over silly secrets about men."

"Silly secrets about men?"

"Dad!"

"Come on, Avila, you're overreacting. I'd hardly call a vampire Claiming Ceremony a marriage."

Her face darkened as she turned on me. "And to make matters worse, you're being a total douche about the whole thing."

Douche?

I was charmed to the point that my feet stopped moving. "This entire city is brimming with vampire douchebags and you're choosing to give yourself to douche-blood-bag supreme himself. How do you expect me to respond?"

She gave a low hiss. "Geez, I don't know, dad. How about inserting a dose of support in your stuffy vamp suit?"

Her hair almost hit my face as she spun around and

began stalking ahead of me. I took a sharp breath. *Since when was I stuffy?*

I wasn't sure that I wanted to know. I started after her. "For the record, philosophy doesn't necessarily equate with stuffiness."

"No, but the word 'master' might."

I stayed quiet for a moment, keeping her pace as we passed a few kindred. As if it were bad enough that we were having this conversation in public, now we had a few spectators to boot. Two female vampires, pale arms wound around each other, stood smirking on the stairs of a brownstone. *Twilight syndrome.* They were an entitled bunch. I looked ahead.

"This isn't the time or place, Avila."

She said nothing though I tuned into her silent message. We gave each other access to our thoughts occasionally. That was usually when there was something important to share when in the company of the more amusing members of our community. I had to admit that it was a cool gift to possess, though right now, her frustrated plea felt anything but that.

She turned the last corner and entered a narrow laneway that ran along the back of a building. My pace slowed momentarily as she walked ahead. The image of her strutting ahead reminded me of when she was five-years old and I had just told her that her mother was never coming home again.

"Where are you going?" I called.

She spun around and the muted morning light caught her crown. She bit her bottom lip and gestured with her chin to follow her. I resumed walking and saw the little girl who had bit her lip and silently trembled after hearing the words that would change her life. *My little tough nugget.* That was the moment she was reborn into a different kid. Blood would stain her chin before she had finally allowed herself to cry in my arms.

She stopped next to a tacky timber door and looked at me. I glanced at the building that had clearly seen better days. It appeared to be a sporting arena undergoing repair. Scaffolding stretched along the outside.

She began to fidget with the sleeves of her sweater. "I want to show you something."

I nodded and went to follow her inside the building, but my senses snapped before I even crossed the threshold. I frowned as the beginnings of what looked to be an internal barnyard complete with livestock came into view.

What the hell?

The place wafted with the smell of spelt combined with the faint odor of animal waste. The vast space had been gutted and refurbished into a makeshift farm. On the far side of the arena stood a replica of a timber barn house with huge double doors and a pitched roof. There were stables with sheep and horses, as well as chook pens and goats. It all spilled into an outdoor grazing area via an enormous roller door. A wheat-colored hen closely tailed by her chicks waddled by as Avila turned to look at me. She tossed her head and folded her arms. Her eyes homed in on me.

"It's for the Leavings. Fresh produce all the way." She gestured beyond. "He even has plans to grow crops along the outside perimeter of the dome so he can feed them the best. He's sending out men each night to begin sanctioning and securing the fields off."

I stepped closer to her. "And why do you think that is, Avila?"

She frowned. "He's not as bad as you think. He wants to find his heart again and I'm the way. I make him *feel* something, Dad. Don't you see that I can make a difference as the vampire queen?"

I held her gaze and my stomach churned. *She believed in him.* I shifted my gaze on a wiry goat chewing on a stick of hay. "Do you love him?"

Her reply was everything I didn't want to hear.

"I do."

9

CRYPTIC LOOKING GAME

"Thank you for joining me, Jett."

Marius leaned back on his French Provincial chair across the table and grinned. *Game.* It was written all over his face. His thick hair was as glossy as the black satin sleeves slipping down to his elbow as he motioned toward a woman who lingered in the shadows on the far side of the saloon. "We have much to discuss."

News to me.

Discussion with Marius in the Crypt was the last thing I desired but I had no choice. The overlord had summoned me. I gave a brief nod and looked away.

We sat in a large room that Marius called his saloon. It was a stately affair with a sophisticated vibe. The elaborately framed artwork and sculptured furnishings created elegance. Too bad the charm didn't extend to my host.

"What do you think?"

I looked back at him. "About…?"

He gestured around. "The Crypt, of course."

"Of course."

The Crypt was really an old stone cathedral created by our ancestors. It had been a famous icon of the old world. He was currently transforming it to make it more homely. If that was possible. I focused on the woman as she busied herself with a crystal decanter and two silver goblets.

"The renovations are coming along superbly. You must be pleased."

"Yes I am. Anything to appease my beloved. She certainly has an interesting and strong mind." He laughed. "I admire her very much."

It hurt to nod. *Avila.* She was to live here. I tried not to grimace.

"She's been encouraged to be herself."

"I am forever indebted to you."

I held his gaze. "You love her?"

"She lights me up on the inside. Everything I do is for her." He leaned forward. "Does that surprise you?"

"No."

The woman approached us. She wore next to nothing and carried a polished tray. Her skin was milky and deliciously smooth, and her long hair blazed red over a boob tube. I couldn't help but notice how her legs paraded beneath a tiny white skirt. All thoughts momentarily evaporated. *Desire.* The animal within ignited.

Marius called them his chamber ladies. He claimed that their presence here supported the new community. A vampire overlord required serving in his private abode. I wondered if my strong-minded daughter shared the same views on his barely clothed servants. I also wondered how far their services extended. Vampires excelled at indulging.

She neared us with a sultry smile. "Gentlemen."

"Thank you, Dana." Marius barely glanced at her as she placed a goblet in front of each of us before filling them with blood. She smelled like a field of lilies and wild sex. I caught the slight shift in her eyes when she looked at me.

"May I get you something else, master?"

I shook my head and looked away. Vampire desires were something to be acknowledged before you could fully master their influence. I wasn't about to indulge. Least of all with one of Marius' chamber ladies. He waited for Dana to leave before speaking again.

"Above all else, it is my desire to keep your daughter safe." His talons wound around his goblet. "That is why I summoned you here."

"Then we are on the same page in that regard, though I find it odd that we're sitting over silver goblets to speak of your love for my daughter." I took a sip of blood. It had been warmed and it was heavenly sweet. This was the new way to feed in Bloodfaye. Marius pushed for a cultivated society. It was better than the alternative. I drummed my talons against the silver stem. "Why am I really here, Marius?"

"Always direct."

"Life's too short not to be."

"Good one." He laughed but I didn't. He set the goblet down. "Are you happy with your living arrangements?"

Game. Here we go.

We both knew that I had been given special privileges since my return from wolf-hunt wilderness. Marius had ensured that I was able to select my preferred dwelling. He claimed it was because I had proved my loyalty to him after my betrayal but we both knew the truth. He needed me on his side for two reasons. We'd just discussed the first.

I shrugged. "Happy is something that belongs in the past. I am satisfied with my living arrangements, thank you."

"You are quite welcome." He gave a stiff smile. "And I trust that you have had time to adjust to the news of the upcoming Claiming Ceremony?"

"Did I have a choice?"

"We all have a choice."

I laughed. "Well, it seems that choice *and* trust are overrated in the new world."

"Perhaps you are right on that score. Though, from one man to another, I can assure you that I have the clan's best interests at heart."

"And what of my daughter's heart?"

He was quiet for a moment. The sound of laughter faintly drifted from other parts of the Crypt. He traced a finger across his brow and switched the subject. "How are things progressing in the lab with the incoming Leavings?"

"If you're referring to testing an AB positive blood type – zero success. However, it is important that the conditions be improved for the Leavings."

"How so?"

"The goal is to offer them a safe place to exist in a vampire-infested world. Their experience here should be somewhat humane from the moment they arrive, especially if you wish for others to seek refuge here by their own freewill … word has a way of leaking." I raised the goblet. "They are, after all, sustaining us."

"Hmm…" He looped his hands around the back of his head. The move was casual yet conveyed a certain amount of power. My senses bristled.

"This *is* something to be considered. You are aware that the Leaving intake process is still developing along with District H living conditions. I will ensure your suggestions are integrated, however, I am about to begin fostering another division of Leavings. I will, of course, require your full co-operation."

Ah, and here comes the meat.

I said nothing and waited for him to elaborate. Though nothing could have prepared me for his next words.

"From this moment on, all present and future Leaving children are to be separated from their parents and taken to District X where they will remain until they reach maturity."

"Say what?" I could feel my face straining. "Since when did Bloodfaye have a District X?"

"Since the beginning. I do not inform you of everything, Jett."

"Apparently. Why?"

His look of self-gratification made my fingertips tingle.

"You haven't figured it out? For a smart guy you can be incredibly dumb."

"So I've been told. What are you going to do with the Leaving children?"

His eyes lit up. "I'm preparing for the future survival of the Mysticus Clan and ensuring the safety of your daughter. That's about all you need to know at this stage."

"You're protecting the Mysticus by taking children from their parents?"

"Yes."

"You can't possibly expect them to survive such an

ordeal after everything they've already endured at the hands of the virus. The children *need* their parents."

"And we *need* to survive. The children will die if they remain in District H. You know they will eventually be taken. Even I cannot always control the supernatural urges of the kindred as much as they cannot control themselves. District X offers them protection and security."

"It offers them an orphanage and a loveless existence!"

He slammed his palms on the table. The oiled timber splintered as he dug in. "This *will* be done, and not only will you comply but one day you will thank me for it and so will Avila."

I regarded the man who had taken my daughter from me and delivered her to hell. He was about to claim her forever. *Hollow hate.* It filled me like dark beauty. I'd rather die than thank him. Of course, now wasn't the time to say as much.

He sat back in his chair. His features were unreadable. I was staring at death. "I'm certain we can get on the same page in regards to this situation too." He paused to ensure he had my full attention. "Of course, we cannot have Zaros discovering this little side project for now, not until I am satisfied with his allegiance to the clan. We both know he presents a risk."

That was true. But Zaros and his unpredictable ways were the last thing on my mind in that moment. As were the children. I nodded. Marius was right about irresistible supernatural urges. Mine was looking game and it felt like a renewed purpose.

I would do whatever it took to stop the Claiming Ceremony.

CRAZY SCIENCE

I clicked my talons against the bench surface as the sound of Michal's voice droned in my ear. He was going on about developing cell culture and cellular layers. It was clear that he was displeased. My nostrils burned. Ethanol stunk like spirited rotting garbage at the best of times and the confined space in our inoculation chamber made the stench almost unbearable.

"Crazy, crazy!" Michal's scrawny shoulders hunched over a set of measuring equipment. He pushed on buttons and scowled before squinting at me. "The voltage across the cellular layers is unstable. I can't determine the correct pathways. In one moment, the junction formations appear tight and confluent, and in the next, they are leaky. I'm going to need more time."

"Which we don't have."

I had already spent hours studying the cell

development and realized that we may have been somewhat ambitious in our presumed timeline. The hybrid blood was composed of many interconnected parts. It was complex and extraordinary. I knew it could take months, if not years, to reach the next step in the process. It was an obstacle I refused to acknowledge out loud. We *did* exist in a new world comprised of new rules.

Michal pushed his glasses up along his damp nose. "But if we are to develop a working recombinant vaccine, we're.…"

"Going to have to improvise." I ignored his gaping jaw and gestured toward the series of cell cultures growing in dishes along the benchtop. They sat among analytical instruments, balancing equipment and titrators. "Must I remind you that this is no ordinary vaccine research?"

"N – no, but it *is* perhaps the most vital research we've undertaken."

I leaned against the bench and eyed him. The sleeves of his lab coat were stained like rust and he appeared more erratic than usual. "What's vital is that this happens before Avila is claimed by our overlord to become a pawn in his dirty power-play games."

"Y – you don't know that that is the case, I'm sure Marius has noble intentions for Avila, as for the future of the clan.."

"Ha." His response was all it took to run hard in my

blood. "If you believe that bullshit then you are as sly as the blood on your sleeves." He was about to speak when I grabbed his collar and wrenched it. "Who the fuck is feeding from you, hmm?"

He trembled and began to stutter. "I – I – I can't stop him."

"Who can't you stop, Michal?"

His eyes twitched as he met my glare. "Z – Zaros."

"Zaros?"

"Yes."

Crafty motherfucker.

I released him and stepped back. He squirmed awkwardly as I regarded him. "Since when?"

"Since whenever he felt like it." He stuffed his hands in his pockets. "I've been their 'pet' from the start; you know this."

Indeed. Yet those kinds of arrangements were meant to cease when we migrated into Bloodfaye. It was the whole point of the bloodletting program. I shoved a palm through my hair. My scalp felt clammy.

"I don't like it."

"What's to like?" he shrugged. "Enduring the bite of the kindred doesn't exactly tickle, you know. B – but there is a way to stop him."

"I'm listening."

"Turn me."

"Now who's crazy, crazy?" I gave a half laugh and started for the antechamber. It was the sheeted off section we had constructed between the room entrance and inoculation chamber which served as an airlock. It wasn't perfect but it served its purpose to create a sterile environment. I paused and looked back at him. "To turn you is defeating the purpose of everything we are trying to accomplish here. Once we have a vaccine to the V-virus, there will be no vampires around to feed on you and call you 'pet'. You'll be free again."

He yelped and flapped his arms in the air. I tried not to smirk. He looked like a cross between a dog and a penguin.

"But that could take too long! We don't know if it will work or if someone will discover our deception before we can even begin to embark on the plasmid construction." He was referring to the next step in the vaccine development – the one I was reluctant to acknowledge. I watched as he paused to gulp some air. "And the vampire gods know we can't do that until the epithelium indicates the presence of tight junctions."

I grinned. "Like I said, we will improvise."

"But even improvisation can't determine the immunogenicity and safety of the vaccine for our candidate. It could be dangerous for him."

"More dangerous than a vampire?" I laughed. "The kid is supernatural now, Michal. We can't damage him any more than I already have."

He looked away. I could tell he was biting back the words. He knew better than to argue with a vampire. His gaze appeared lucid when it finally met mine. "Where are you going?"

"I'm going to find Zaros."

"Oh."

I contemplated him for a moment and saw a man whose heart was filled with fear. "Everything will be okay."

"Okay."

I gave a stiff nod and gripped the flap of the plastic sheeting wall. "Good. I want a trial viral vector ready to transfer to our rat subjects by tomorrow night. Make it happen."

He nodded fast. "Yes master."

"And stop calling me master, would you," I said as I stepped into the antechamber. The thick plastic folded closed behind me and my next breath was ethanol free. My lungs silently rejoiced.

11

BLOODPLAY AT THE MUSEUM

It was white, moved slower than I could run and stunk like rotten eggs. But I couldn't refuse the shiny golf cart parked out front of my brownstone on my return to District V. It was a gift from our lord and master. I knew he meant to butter me up somewhat, but I wasn't feeling overly special because just about every vampire in the city was queued up to get one. I noticed that my cart was swankier than most. It had built-in heated seats. I figured if I sat here long enough, my cold-blooded ass might have a chance of thawing. One could only hope.

I shifted my butt against the warm seat as I set off toward downtown Bloodfaye. It was a delightfully indulgent sensation. I smiled. I'm certain that someone once said it was better to let our hopes and not our hurts shape our future. Well, my ass was full of hope alright, but I knew it was short-lived – I was on my way to see Zaros.

For reasons beyond my comprehension, Zaros and his crew had taken a fancy to the Norbury museum and slept among artifacts and other things formerly preserved for public exhibition. I was familiar with the building as it had been one of Avila's favorite places to visit as a child. We'd spent many hours wandering the halls discussing ancient species and extinct reptiles. She had particularly favored the Smilodon exhibition for their long, curved saber-shaped teeth. *Ha.* It's no wonder she had taken to the new world like a duck to water. Long teeth are all the fashion nowadays.

I focused on the road as I steered the cart through District V's main artery. Vampire folk were out in droves, with the latest fashion trend on display as they pranced around like glow-in-the-dark fireflies. Freak show psychics. Faceless blondes. Wicked civilians. Laughter abounded and irritated the crap out of me. Marius was fast achieving his objective for the Mysticus. It was clear they felt at ease and protected in the dome city.

I swallowed hard and pinched my lips shut. I wasn't sure if I was more disgusted with myself or this entire nice, law-abiding urban affair. As if we hadn't become the definition of demonic force existing comfortably while enslaving humans for their blood. And I was an active participant. I could only hope that respite from this damnation would arrive in the form of tomorrow night's viral vector.

A gangly looking vampire waved me down as I stopped in front of the museum. He was clad in dull worn leather. His hands resembled chopsticks and his face raw sewage and partially hidden beneath dark glasses. He was quick to cramp up my personal space as soon as I alighted from the cart. I backed away. I hated people getting too close and he emitted like a postman's sock.

"Master Jett." He planted his feet wide but his pockmarked jaw slackened. "Err… do you have business with … um … Lord Zaros?"

What is this – the evacuated Twilight security clan?

"Clearly I didn't come here for my health."

He went to say something, but I ignored him and started for the wide set of stairs leading toward the museum entrance. I tried not to flinch when he fell into step beside me.

"The Lord isn't … err … taking unsolicited guests right now."

"Unsolicited? That's a big word." I took the stairs two at a time and kept my eyes on the twin glass doors of the museum. *Awesome.* It was security clan free. "Not to worry; I'm sure Zaros is expecting me."

"He – he didn't say as much." He side-stepped in front of me as we reached the landing. His lofty figure blocked the entrance as he adopted a business-like expression. "I'm going to have to ask you to wait here so I can get the lowdown from Zaros."

I shrugged. "You've got to do what you've got to, huh?"

Saliva pooled on his bottom lip. "Err … yeah … I guess."

He interpreted my comment as cooperation and gave a nod before bony fingers hooked over the brass handle and pushed open the door. I didn't give him the chance to make good on his word and shoved past him and into the lobby, my boots squeaking on the tiles when I paused to sniff out Zaros.

"Oi!" The dweeb-guy rushed up behind and grabbed my elbow. "What the fuck do ya think ya doing?" he hissed.

Spoiled innards. Vampires had foul breath at the best of times.

"Back off, dweeb."

I shoved a palm into his chest, snapping his ribs like crispy sugar peas. He stumbled back and I returned his hiss in the most vicious way possible.

"Touch me again and I'm looking for your heart."

He slurped back the running drool from his lip and clawed his palms but said nothing as a chorus of laughter erupted from unseen corridors to reverberate all around. *Bloodplay.* It was just the beginning. My nerves chilled as I looked around the lobby. The walls stretched with shadows in the wake of a few discreet downlights, barely illuminating the pterodactyl bones that suspended from the highly slanted ceiling. The skeleton appeared grotesque, hollow, and chalky. To my left was the patently vacant counter.

"Ha. You really do have a heart fetish, master J."

Zaros strode into the lobby like a slinking panther and he was wearing a pair of chrome buckled leathers that hung loosely above his groin. Some of his crew trailed behind him. My nose swelled. He smelled like a cocktail of sweat and semen and wore nothing else but the ink staining his bare chest.

He stopped short of me. "Losing your own love-Gucci so soon?"

Chutzpah.

"The devil wears Prada these days."

The two blood-gangers lingering behind Zaros laughed. I recognized them from our recent subway rendezvous – the green-eyed schmuck and the straw-haired scarecrow. Throw them in an exhibit and call it human evolution turned vile.

"Iconic," Zaros said. His black stare zeroed in on dweeb-guy. "Really, Isaac?"

"I …. err …. um …. he got inside, master."

"Clearly."

Isaac wiped his leaky mouth with the back of his hand. "I'm sorry. I …."

Zaros held up a palm to silence him. His voice was

like knives. "Get back out there and try putting in some big dick energy in ya fucking job, yes?"

"Yeah – B. D. E. M." Green-eyes grabbed his balls and gave a thrust for good measure. "Moron."

Scarecrow laughed. Isaac sneered. Zaros dismissed the scene with a flick of his wrist. "Leave us!"

He was silent as the three vampires left then he turned and glared at me. "Why are you here?"

"Michal."

"*Your* pet?" His fangs glinted like the bones hovering above us. "Now, that is a surprise."

"He is not my pet nor is he yours."

He gave a wide gesture with his arms and laughed. "Ah, but the world is now full of devils who wear Prada and human blood-smooches, don't you agree?"

"No."

"Marius has created the perfect conditions for such a package and from where I'm standing, you be shipping with it, *doc*."

"I'd be shipping better when you give me your word to leave Michal well alone."

He laughed. "Ludicrous!" His skin appeared darkly fluid as he started to ramble. "A vampire's word is not gospel, but it might suffice to hold if you are willing to stand beside me." He paused. "I know your undead heart still pumps for humanity. You resent the way the Leavings are being treated in Bloodfaye."

Ugh. Incoming vampire verbal diarrhea.

My forehead began to throb. I gave him a look that must have encouraged him to continue. The shit factor didn't disappoint.

"Listen doc, I'm with you. This vampire master is outraged about Marius' plans to enforce slavery on our Leavings. Is it not enough that we drain their blood every couple of months to satisfy our thirst?" He paused and thumped his chest. "History and white men were never kind to my people. The world has changed, and we've been given a clean slate, but Marius wishes to recreate treacherous old pathways in the form of fascism and subjugation. Damn! The dick wants to bring back slavery! It isn't right."

"And you're suggesting ....?"

"Freedom for all."

I laughed. "Delusional."

"Why?"

"Because the world is blood-driven and as much as I reject human slavery, those Leavings are safer in the dome than out in the wild."

It was true. We might be the only vampires currently dominating this town but it was foolish to believe that other clans would not eventually try to stake our territory and our humans. And it wasn't as if humans were currently in large supply.

Zaros' nostrils flared so wide that I almost caught a glimpse of his brain. He placed a talon over his belt and studied me. "There is another way."

"Enlighten me."

"Help me overthrow Marius and ensure my place as Bloodfaye's sole overlord, and I will make sure all Leavings are given a real choice – they can come and go as they please so long as they agree to take part in the bloodletting program."

"Sounds ideal but you're forgetting one vital thing – their freedom will bring anarchy and more death. We're dealing with a horde of carnivorous creatures whose dead hearts live to hunt and kill humans. As it is, Marius has succeeded in establishing civility to the clan – at least for those beneath the dome. Freedom for the Leavings will stoke the primal urges of every vampire in Norbury city. They won't be safe; they'll become prey again."

Zaros stepped closer. His breath crept over my face like a rancid cockroach.

"These are the times to be thinking hard about which direction you and your *pet* be shipping." His eyes drilled into me. "Especially considering that your girl is, by default, about to become a prime target as the vampire queen."

I clenched. "Is that a threat, *master*?"

His upper lip curled to reveal pearly tusks. "Call it what you want blood-sap, but if I were you, I'd be calling it the right way."

Bloodplay. He had delivered and it was violence I felt calling me in that moment. I took a deliberate breath and forced myself to think about bananas. I didn't come here for brutality, and I sure as hell couldn't eat a banana. Not for one moment did I believe his intentions for the Leavings to be noble, particularly when accompanied with dirty intimidation. He sought supremacy and nothing more.

I was about to say as much when the familiar, sweet sound of angel-minx filled the room. My jaw felt like led when I saw Sun striding toward us. Her pale skin revealed more color than usual, and I noticed a distinct sensual sway to her hips.

What the hell is she doing here?

"Jett." She stopped next to Zaros. They exchanged a lingering look before her eyes settled on me. Her hair shone like golden vine. "How very unusual to see you here."

I gave a half laugh and looked at Zaros. "Love-Gucci found."

12

DREAMING OF YOU

"Daddy, I've got a secret!" Avila rushed toward me and flung herself in my arms. Giggles like popping corn muffled against my sweater. I stroked the back of her head. The dewy air clung to her after having just returned home from an outing with her mother. Bright eyes peered up at me. "Do you want to see?"

"Of course, I want to see."

"Avila." Melissa appeared at the threshold of my office. She tried to smile as she leaned against the door frame. "Daddy is working right now. Let's show him your secret later."

Avila wriggled free. Her nose crinkled as she began to pull off her coat. "But I want to show him now."

"It's okay, little nugget, you *can* show me now." I looked at Melissa and mouthed a "Hey you".

She normally responded to our love language but not

today. She frowned before going to our daughter. I leaned into my chair and watched as she helped Avila remove her woolen coat. The distraction was welcome. Blood diagnostics and mineral content graphs were clogging my brain like sloppy discharge.

Avila's undershirt momentarily stretched and slipped from her shoulder as she shrugged off her coat. The scene slowed down long enough for me to spot the plaster fixed on Avila's upper arm as Melissa readjusted her sleeves and softly chided: "Remember what we talked about when it comes to secrets?"

"Yes Momma."

Melissa dropped her head to the side and gave me a coy smile. Her upper lip lifted, and her face flickered. *Bones.* Her skull blinked at me. Then it was gone when she turned to whisper in Avila's ear. The vibe was like an echo. I tried to speak but couldn't. It was then that Avila spun around. Her vibrant skirt cut through my brain with her fast twirl as she bolted from the room.

"Be right back!"

It took all my will to speak. "What was that all about?"

"What?"

"Secrets."

A dark grin and my tiny hairs raised.

"She's got a secret."

"Yeah, so she said."

Melissa's face glitched. "She's got a *special* secret, Jett."

"Melissa?" I managed to stand up. "Is everything okay?"

"Nothing is okay."

Avila came back into the room. "Daddy, meet Shana!"

"Sha–" I was looking at a wolf.

I tried to refocus. The wolf's gray gaze was like a moment of serenity amid a twine of sterling fur. Her coat glossed in the waning sunlight offered by the window behind me. Peculiarity just hit its stride. I collected my bottom lip as Avila clawed her fingers through the wolf's mane and laughed.

"Mommy said that I could keep her, but I must keep her a secret because she's super, super special."

Melissa stroked Avila's forehead. "*Our* super special secret."

"A very special secret."

"Between you and me," Melissa said.

"And Daddy!"

I shuddered. My two girls felt like strangers and there was a wolf in my office called Shana whose eyes spoke secrets of their own. *Shana.* The name circled my head like a lazy siesta. I was grasping at straws.

"Wait – a wolf?"

"Remember what I told you? There are no accidents, Jett." Melissa turned abruptly. Her thin arms flailed like a mad woman. "Secrets become death and death becomes poison!"

Hello.

Nothing made sense, and yet, everything made sense. Realism set in my bones even as I became aware of my lucid dream state. Messages from the dead kept me on my toes. Shana was the half breed Lygarou whose blood I was working with Michal. Melissa had brought her into my dream. *Why?* Nothing was normal about the new normal.

I tried to regain balance. It *was* my dream. Control was within reach. I fingered my chin to help harness clarity. An odd sense of time warp snapped my awareness as I held Melissa's stare.

"What secrets are you talking about? Shana's blood?"

"No."

It was strange talking to the dead in your dreams. She was real but not. The next real thing I knew was Avila's scream as she was lifted off her feet. Her legs kicked wildly as an unseen force held her suspended in the air.

"Daddy!"

"Avila!"

So much for dream control. Some dreams felt more real than what we call reality. Avila's screams escalated. I let out a frenetic growl and went to move but my boots were nailed to the floor.

What the?

Delusion was control. The room shrouded into

darkness. The enemy wasn't in sight, but it was present and powerfully demonic. Every one of my nerve endings stood on end. Fear provoked hostility. My calf muscles squeezed as I strained to move. I knew evil like second skin, but this invisible entity was Satan. Every part of me knew it.

Avila called out. My name sounded like a chilling crossword clue. Melissa reached for Avila. Primitive instinct overdrive and a wrangled snarl. *Nightmare.* It was as wicked as the bright flash in the corner of my eye. Avila's back teeth ground like needles in my ear as a shadow above her began to take form and the air was suffused with the vile and eerie.

Wayward genies and perverted ogres. Everything went askew. A hellion eye hung like the sullied. *Succubus.* Melissa screamed and Avila was gone. *Gone.* Shana's doleful howl filled the hollow before silence.

Melissa's haunting voice followed me into wakefulness. *"She has a secret, Jett; a special secret."*

13

DRAVEN SANGUISA

A usual laboratory work day of blood-hype hustle and foul mouths was beginning to wind down with no dead Leavings to report. It would count as a good day if they still existed. A few Mysticus scientists and guards remained scattered throughout the workshop. Bleach and solvent vapors irritated my senses as I glanced at the Leaving man sitting next to me before pricking a syringe into his flesh. He was among the last bloods scheduled for the day, and honestly, I barely noticed him.

I was almost immune to the fresh heartbeats cruising through bloodwork central. Humans appeared the same of late – skin and bone, and fermented hatred that reeked of saline. At least their bodily stench had been eradicated. Marius had made good on his word and implemented a cleansing process prior to giving all Leavings a bed in what was called the Segregation Hall.

The Segregation Hall was an old school gym transformed into a giant dormitory where they secured Leavings before scheduling them for bloodwork. They were then assigned quarters in District H provided their blood was clean. Diseased Leavings were denied entry into Bloodfaye. We had no use for contaminated blood. The Mysticus avoided sickness at all costs and had learned the hard way. Greedy kindred peeling from the inside out had paved the way for us. Diseased blood was a potential vampire killer.

Aside from taking the blood of Leavings, Marius was also commissioning another pass for the incomings in the form of a physical assessment which was set to take place in the Diversion Yard. Basically, we would be able to determine their slave-value factor and thus assign them to suitable jobs. I figured those Leavings who were out of shape would be thrown back into the ruined city with the diseased humans and outcast kindred. Yes, not every Norbury city vampire had made it into Bloodfaye. Some kindred proved too weak in the face of their supernatural cravings and desires. Their rebellious nature could not be controlled even by the vindictive likes of Marius. We called them the Cruentus.

Rebellion was a long-running theme nowadays. The Segregation Hall had become the pulse for Leaving gang bangers and hawkers to wreak havoc over their weaker counterparts. Even a vampire apocalypse couldn't snub man's deep-seated need for power and coercion. Humans. Vampires. Lygarou. Witches. It didn't matter which skin we now wore. The feeble were always going to be abused and monopolized.

The Leaving man jolted me from my idle thoughts when he cleared his throat. I didn't look at him when I replaced the puncture wound with a cotton pad and instructed him to apply pressure. His voice croaked as I went for some white tape.

"So, what's it like on the other side, doc?"

"It's heaven on earth."

"Really?"

"No." I tore a piece of tape and stuck it over the cotton pad. I looked at him and saw a young man with a lost future whose copper eyes flecked blue over deep shadows. I shrugged. "But if you play it smart and follow the rules, you've got a better chance at survival than out there."

"Any chance they'll turn me?"

"No."

He chuckled. "Didn't think so."

"You can make it in the new world if you keep your head down and wait it out."

"Nice advice coming from the top of the food chain."

I grinned. "Depends on how you look at it. Our survival depends on yours. So, who *really* tops the food chain, hmm?"

He looked beyond me as the distinct sound of heels tapped on the tiles from some place behind. "Now, vamps like her can top my food chain anytime."

Feline rabbit holes. Man's everlasting mystery that the apocalypse couldn't annihilate either. Such is the nature of the supernatural alike. I didn't need to turn around to know her identity. I could detect Sun's angel-minx scent a mile away. Particularly now that she burned with Zaros' sex between her thighs.

Her touch on my shoulder was electric. "Master Jett, are you ready for our meeting?"

"Just about."

I copped an eyeful of blazing amber and my heart almost seared to ashes. I deliberately avoided looking at her tight blouse and dropped my gaze to take in the black shiny knee-highs skimming up her calves. She was more distracting than usual. Feline rabbit holes indeed. I wasn't jumping in. I turned to dismiss the human.

"Close your mouth and move on, Leaving."

His pulse throbbed in my ear as I motioned for a nearby Mysticus guard to escort him away. A white leather clad guard stepped up pronto. He was unusually tall and barrel chested for an Asian man-cum-vampire, and his skin showed fading pitted scars.

The Leaving man grazed a hand over his scalp and laughed as he stood up. "Nah. She be my Desdemona."

"Ha." Sun gripped her hips as the guard grabbed the Leaving's elbow and gave a good yank. He stumbled back, but he kept his eyes on Sun and grinned. She shook her head. "You are no Othello, Leaving."

"I can be any kind of Shakespeare that you want me to be; just name it, honeypot."

Sun burst out laughing. The guard scowled and shoved the Leaving with a snarl. "Watch your mouth, cockbag."

"Alright, alright! I'm watching." The Leaving man flailed his arms and moved forward with the guard shadowing him until they reached an exit door a little way along the aisle. It didn't stop him from sneaking a quick wink at Sun before he was pushed from the lab entirely.

Sun's laugh was all breath and no sound.

"It's nice to see some of them are still spirited." She smoothed her skirt. "He should have gone with Juliet."

I shut down the workstation computer and stood. "Don't tell me you are a sucker for dying love?"

We started walking the aisle between the long stretches of pristine white benchtops that were our workstations. The lab was empty now, allowing us to talk in private. I had a few things to say.

"I think all of us are suckers for dying love these days."

"Perhaps more of us than others."

She curled a lock of hair over her ear and glanced at me. "It's not what you think, Jett."

"What do I think?"

"That I am making a mistake with Zaros."

I glanced up at the square oyster lights mounted flush against the ceiling. "He's catfishing you without the social media part, Sun. He's deceptive and dangerous. You need to stop sleeping with him."

"Excuse me?" She scowled. "You're getting way too big for your vampire boots. I don't answer to you or anyone, *Master J*."

"Dumbest thing I ever heard you say."

There was someone I was eager to meet waiting on the other side of the door at the end of the aisle. That's why she'd come here. "None of us are free in the new world. You know this."

Her boots clicked behind me like the passion in her voice.

"They can't take away our freedom to love."

I fixed my stare on the large chrome door a few meters from me. "You love him?"

"N – no!"

She smelled like a woman in love. And if there was anything that I knew about a woman in love, it was that she was loyal to her heart. I turned to meet her fiery eyes.

"You're a part of the resistance, Sun. Screwing the enemy compromises your allegiance to our cause." I gestured toward the door. "You are risking everything that we have been doing to reverse the damage inflicted by the V-Virus – and for what? A supercharged orgasm?"

"My allegiance to the secret sector is as solid as ever.

For you to even question my loyalty to you is barbarous." She paused and inhaled sharply. "It's just sex and nothing more."

"Then make it nothing more." I ignored whatever response she was about to throw at me and strode toward the door, briefly looking back at her as I gripped the handle. She swallowed visibly beneath my stare. "Is he informed and prepared for his part in the viral transfer?"

"Yes."

"Good."

I pulled on the door handle to reveal the image of a male vampire sprawled across the bench seat that butted against the wall of the building's entrance. Long hair the color of mud contrasted against the white of his shirt, while his knees rested bent against the wall and appeared swamped in a pair of baggy jeans. He jerked to his feet in an instant, scraping a hand through his hair and bounding toward me with a twitchy grin. His voice was unsteady.

"Master Jett?" His shoulders lifted with his sudden laugh. "Sire, I have been waiting to meet you."

"And I you. Let me apologize for our delayed introduction, things have been a little hectic of late."

"Oh, totally fine, dude – I – I mean, sire." He started to pull at the hem of his T-shirt. His eyes darted between me and Sun as she came up next to me. "I want to thank you for saving my life back in the subway."

God. Is that what he thought I did?

I didn't know that I agreed, but I wasn't letting him in

on that piece of intel. "You are very welcome. Sun tells me that you are all set to undergo your transition back to humanity in the coming days. I am pleased that you have accepted your vital role in bringing normality back to the world and thereby saving many lives. You are to be commended for your courage."

He nodded rapidly. "I am at your service, sire. Whatever you want."

"Hmm – Sun tells me you have a name?"

"Draven Sanguisa."

"Sanguisa?"

"Yeah, my Pop was Latino."

"Well." I clasped a hand on his shoulder and smiled. "I am certain that all who remain in the world will soon come to know of a kid who goes by the Latino name Sanguisa."

His dark eyes glittered like a night sky. "Whoa! That is totally cool."

Yeah. Totally.

14

BY MY SIDE

"In the dark of night. Those small hours, I'm uncertain and anxious. I need to call you."

I whispered the song lyrics and a part of me wanted to break. Avila's voice drifted from another room along with the haunting strains of the old INXS track *By My Side*. She had her Bluetooth speaker connected. We were thriving on electricity in the blood-dome as some kindred were skilled tradespeople. I often wondered if they'd ever achieve lighting up the web again. It wasn't in the foreseeable future.

I wish you were so close to me.

The song had been one of Scarla's favorites. I sank back into the living room sofa and inhaled. I whiffed the charred woody remnants of Palo Santo and tangy furniture polish. The scent of Avila's incense sticks clung to every nook and cranny in our home. She said it was to cleanse our space of negative influences and bad energy. She said it provided spiritual protection. I didn't resist her reasonings and rituals – were vampires capable of connecting to anything remotely spiritual? The wicked didn't deserve protection from an omnipresent higher being. But my girl still needed to believe in something good. Her life overflowed with dark nasties and I was one of them.

Scarla never was.

By my side. I wish you were. I wish you were.

Soul-stealer. I still thought of my lover every day. My soul yearned to be closer to her and even though I felt her essence within me, it was never enough. I vaguely looked at the reading nook across the way. The stained white timber panels were reminiscent of Louisiana French flair with their arched French windows and overstuffed cushions that scattered over the broad padded seat below the bookshelves. I saw none of it. I only saw Scarla – the part of me that wanted to break.

Breathe Jett.

It was all I could do to keep from losing my mind over her absence from my life. That and focusing on dispelling the plague that had inevitably taken her from me. At least in my humanity I would escape an eternal life without her. Maybe I deserved this everlasting hell. I wasn't always an angel in my mortality.

Was I doing the right thing?

I knew the repercussions were high enough to claim my life sooner rather than later. If the viral vector reversed the effects of the V-Virus tonight, I planned on reproducing the strain and slipping it into the clan's blood supply. Marius would have my heart for sure. Let him have it.

"Hello, earth to Dad?"

I startled as Avila laughed and walked into the room. "Where were you just now?"

She wore an ivory satin gown like second skin and high strappy sandals. Her toenails were painted scarlet. I had to take a second to collect my jaw. "Right here, baby girl." She looked so …. womanly. I was disturbed. "Wh-what are you wearing?"

Her eyes dropped to the floor and she smiled before looking back at me. "What do you think?"

My mind raced and my gut turned to vinegar. Obviously, the revealing outfit was for the Claiming Ceremony.

"Isn't it a bit.…" I gnawed back my words when her vulnerability hit me hard. I forced a smile. "You look beautiful."

"Really?"

"Yes. You look your mom."

She pushed a hand through her dark hair. "That can't be a bad thing."

"Your mom was a stunning woman. You couldn't go wrong with genes like that."

She grinned and performed a slow pirouette. "Do you think she'd like it?"

I cleared my throat and thought about last night's dream scene. It was better than thinking about her wearing that gown.

"I have no doubt. Listen, odd question – do you remember the time when your mom took you out for the day not long before she died?"

She stopped moving. "She took me places all the time."

"Yes, but this particular time you may have come home with a plaster on your arm. Did you get hurt? Do you recall?"

"I was only young, Dad. I don't know. How come?"

"No reason."

She snorted. "Liar."

I was silent for a moment. Avila didn't know about my secretive activities and alternative plans for the impending extinction of the Mysticus clan, and I wanted to keep it that way. Knowledge like that meant risk and I wasn't jeopardizing her safety for all the blood in the world. Nor did I wish to cause her alarm.

She sat down on the coffee table in front of me. Her skin was like ice when she reached for my hand. "What's going on, Dad?"

"I've been having strange dreams."

"Of Mom?"

"Yeah."

She frowned. "Me too. I didn't want to mention because they have been—"

"Disturbing?"

"Yeah."

Interesting. Extremely.

I leaned forward. "Do you remember the details?"

"As if it happened for real. She shows me death and mayhem, and she keeps repeating the same messages." Avila pulled her hand away and began fidgeting. "She says that I have a secret and there are no—"

"Accidents."

"Exactly! I don't know what she means or what she wants. I mean, I can sense this desperation and then I think it's just me experiencing the pre-wedding jitters, you know?"

I scowled. "I don't know, because you're not getting married."

"What?" She stood with hands on hips.

I groaned inwardly. *Big mouth.* Like I needed to address this battle right before a deceptive life changing and potentially life threatening event.

"I thought we cleared this up?"

"Give me a break. Old habits die hard."

"Well you better find a way to bury them because the ceremony date has been changed to the next full moon."

"Huh?" I blanked out for a second. Her face was a puzzle before I seized back my thoughts. "But that's in a few days. Why the sudden push forward?"

"Four to be exact. Marius doesn't want to wait for the following full moon. We've waited long enough."

"B-but, what's with the full moon deal? We're not werewolves or witches."

"And we're not human either, Dad. Haven't you noticed the power that accompanies each full moon?" She chuckled. "It creeps under your skin and merges with our blood. We are an ancient species, mythical creatures of the night now. Immortals."

No shit. Not for long, baby girl.

"I can feel it, though I don't see why the Claiming Ceremony needs to take place on a full moon night. It's not like it will make a difference."

I could play ignorant when it suited. Resistance did it every time.

She blew back a strand of hair that had fallen over her lips. "It makes all the difference and you know it. We're linked with the earth's elements like never before! It's like discovering and connecting to an incredible version of our existence. You have to honor it, Dad."

"You're passionate like your mom too."

She gave a halfhearted laugh. "You once said that we can't stop change. Don't you think it's about time you stopped fighting this?"

"We should never stop fighting for what we want."

"And what do you want, Dad?"

I wanted my little girl back. I needed my soul lover in my arms again.

Avila's eyes homed in on me like crystallized darts. I looked away. *Was I doing the right thing? Could I change it for the better?* The inner conflict was a wrangle between old and new worlds. It was also torment. My neck was stiff when I looked back at her.

"I want you to be happy."

"That's the easy part. You've just got to let it go and deal with the reality. You are a vampire and I am going to be the vampire queen. Embrace your gifts and your part in it."

I stood up and stroked her cheek with the backs of my fingers. Her smooth white skin reminded me of a geisha. A phantom geisha.

"It's important that you try very hard to remember what happened that day when you came home with a plaster on your arm when you were little." I nodded as she frowned. "Do you think you can do that?"

"You think it matters?"

"Yes."

"Okay, I can try."

"Good." I turned and made for the door, stopping at the threshold when she called after me.

"Where are you going?"

I shrugged. "I'm going to do what you suggested."

"And what's that?"

"Embrace my part in the new world."

She half laughed. "Whatever."

I smirked. "You do look beautiful in that gown."

She nodded and I left the room with my insides churning with quiet desperation.

Well, I wish you were so close to me.

No wishes could bring Scarla into my arms again, but I could do something about my daughter. My nerves were on fire as time slipped away from me. I was on my way to the subway lab to kick V-Virus ass. I didn't want immortality.

Was I doing the right thing?

The choice was out of my hands. This was the path that was notched deep in my undead bones. I couldn't acquiesce to a vampire who had stolen my daughter's humanity and screws with humans for his own power-hungry vampire agenda. Avila's future was worth fighting for. And so was my return to a human heart that could break.

In the dark of night, these faces they haunt me.

15

STEEL DUST PROMISES

"Are you sure this is what you want to do?"

Sun's talons were needles in my arm as we stopped short of the inoculation chamber. We were as deep in the subway as the old steel dust clinging in my nose. I met her stare.

"Second thoughts?"

"It's not my call."

"Not true. You are just as much a part of this as me." I pried her fingers from my arm. Her hand felt jittery. "Or are you?"

"What is that supposed to mean?"

I shrugged. "I'm not the one sleeping with the enemy."

"Who I go to bed with is my business. What you need to think about is the fact that what we're about to do cannot be undone. Marius forgave us once; he won't overlook this if it goes to shit." She shook her head. "He will kill us."

I laughed. "Is shit such a bad thing?"

She was about to reply when the sound of footsteps carried along the subway shaft. She looked away as Lena and one of her crew came into view. They were here to keep watch over the door while the so-called 'shit' was going down.

Hello, Latino Shadow Guardian.

She almost made it all better. I think it was her stark human *in-your-face* qualities. She reminded me of spirit. I watched as Lena stalked toward us in a pair of dirty denims and a matching jacket. Her chunky boots were scuffed, and a worn leather whip was slung at her waist.

"Master Jett. Reporting for rebel duty." She flipped her canary colored ponytail as she stopped in front of me and poked a thumb toward the man beside her. "You know Jamie?"

"Lena." She smelled of summer spunk and the spearmint gum between her jaws. It was nothing new. I acknowledged Jamie with a nod. She was right in that I was familiar with the buff middle aged man with a hot score on his back. I knew his past enough to know that vampires had wiped out his family. He was good for the resistance. His eyes spoke of war and hatred.

I motioned to the lab door behind me. "If anyone

comes down here, knock on the door but under no circumstances enter the room beyond. Got it?"

Lena's expression dimmed. "How come?"

"It's a contamination thing. The same applies if you hear anything going down on the other side – don't open up."

"Hear anything like what?"

I laughed. "You know, wrangled screams—beasty, contorted growls, mystical chanting."

"Why do I feel like I'm a part of a screwed-up version of a horror movie?"

I grinned and grabbed the door handle. "Because you're now living the Hollywood dream, sweetheart."

"Ha. Some dream."

Her retort followed me and Sun into the inoculation chamber, though it was just as fast out of my mind as I pulled on my lab coat and offered Sun a disposable blue smock. We stood between the lengths of sheet plastic that constituted a makeshift airlock chamber. I regarded her as she fastened the smock at her waist.

"You didn't answer my question before."

"You didn't answer mine."

"I'm here, aren't I?"

"Same."

She looked at the flipside of the plastic wall separating us from the lab. Draven's lofty figure slouched on a stool while Michal whizzed around him, taking his vitals. Their images appeared fluid through the plastic.

"I just want you to be sure that this is the right thing."

Am I doing the right thing?

I had made a choice to push tonight's planned trial viral vector to the real deal. Draven would now be receiving the injection in replace of a lab rat. The changed Claiming Ceremony date meant that I was out of time and hope had never looked so crucial. I took a breath and reached for the plastic flap. "I don't know what's right or wrong anymore. I just know that I have to try."

I parted the flap and walked into the chamber before she could answer. The stringent vapors of ethanol greeted me along with Michal's skitzy glance from his position in front of Draven, stethoscope ear tubes jammed in his ears as he pressed the chest piece against Draven's skin.

"Game on. Are we all set?" I said as I approached.

Draven scratched his ear and laughed. Michal scrunched his nose in concentration. I examined the viral cultures and microbial strains that sat in glass dishes along the benchtop as I waited for him to finish.

Michal pulled the tubes from his ears and looked at me. His eyes appeared as big as Garfield's through his thick glasses. "We're as set as the unstable cellular layers; how's that for you?"

"We're dealing with blood that originated from witchcraft. I doubt we'll ever achieve confluence and formation of tight junctions – Works just fine for me. Do you have the viral vector ready for transfer?"

"I've developed a working recombinant and loaded it into the microprocessor controlled injector. Bu-but—"

I interjected. "Good," and gestured toward the tidy cot we had managed to bring in undetected. It wasn't exactly the ideal medical style of bed to suit our needs given the circumstances, but it was a bed nonetheless.

"Draven, why don't you go take a load off?"

Draven rubbed his chin and glanced at the bed. The mattress was covered with white cotton topped with a stained lumpy pillow. It was butted up against the far side of the plastic wall of the room. Not that it was that far considering the room resembled a miasma matchbox.

His throat rolled as he swallowed visibly. "Wh-what's going to happen to me tonight?"

Sun moved between us before I could reply. She looked at me as she spoke to him. "It's just like we talked about, remember?"

"Yeah, but what if it doesn't work?"

I smiled. "The worst that could happen is nothing. You are much stronger than your human self. I mean, you are an immortal being for crying out loud. Our vaccine formula is essentially a reproduction of the same properties that already flow in your blood, with an added twist of a developed version of the V-Virus."

"The wolf bloods?"

"Yeah, the wolf bloods. Which means you will not die tonight, promise."

He nodded. "Alright, I trust you, doc."

"Gratitude."

The word barely formed as he slinked from the stool and followed Sun to the cot while I sucked in a breath. I'd just delivered a promise knowing that promises made by the undead remained undead.

I let out a long breath and watched Sun stroke his forehead and offer soothing words.

Why did I do that?

It was the part of me that believed in the path. This little shindig had to pay off. I palmed my throbbing head as Michal's discomforting words thumped against my temples.

He gripped the stethoscope tube that hung around his neck. "Ho-how can you be so certain that we'll do him no harm when we're working like blind mice running up to the farmer's wife? I-I-I think we should wait until we know it's the right thing to do."

"It *is* the right thing to do." I grabbed the microprocessor injector from the bench. "His vitals?"

"Sta-stable. How do you know?"

This question made my headache worse. Did no one else get it?

"Listen, my daughter is about to belong to a blood-sucking fiend who can't see past his supernatural inflated ego; humans are being treated as blood-cow slaves and innocent children are currently being removed from their parents to one day become soulless immortal puppets to soulless king puppeteer himself –

we have in our hands the solution to stop all of this before it gets worse."

I paused and regarded his frigid expression before stepping closer. "That's how I know. Can we get this done now?"

"Yes master."

"Awesome."

The following moments played out like a scene from who knows what. Injecting a viral vector into someone's bloodstream was far from extraordinary and Draven was an ideal candidate. He was a young, healthy vampire who took the injection without incident then rested while we kept an eye on his vitals.

I expected his transformation back to humanity to be much like transitioning into vampirism – an uneventful transaction between life and death.

He would have to die to reawaken in his human form. Too bad the atmosphere in the inoculation chamber couldn't die and be reborn along with him. It was that tense.

"What now?"

Sun and I exchanged glances as I leaned against the bench while Michal fussed over Draven, taking his vitals with various instruments. Sun perched on the stool fiddling with the hem of her smock.

"We wait."

She groaned. "This place gives me the creeps."

"What? You don't like what we've done with the joint?" I grinned. "That blue suits you."

She scowled. "Yeah well, don't get used to it. I don't plan to come back in here."

"You're too lovely to be a scientist anyway."

She laughed. "Is that what I am these days?"

"You're still like the sun when there's no sun, *Sun.*"

We both smiled and I went to touch her twilight skin when Michal gasped and whirled around to look at us.

"His heart has stopped! It's working!"

"Hello, hello."

I pushed off the bench and went to the bedside, with Sun close behind. I noticed Draven's talons recede and his skin become plump pink like the living as he slept. His breath kickstarted and then deepened.

Sun grabbed my arm. "He's human again!"

Yes!

I laughed as Michal squealed. The shindig *had* paid off and now we could begin the next phase of eradicating the V-Virus from the world.

Humanity would be ours again. I felt like singing with angels and was about to say as much when Draven groaned. He convulsed violently for few a moments.

Sun grabbed my arm. "What's happening?"

Draven abruptly stilled. My nerves were like sharp knives. His eyes flew open to settle on me as I peered back into dark demon red. Realization dawned and Draven's skin turned to mottled yellow putrefaction.

He opened his jaw and growled like a hungry beast as his beady eyes flicked toward Michal. Sun's gasp nipped at my ears as Draven sat up and grinned. His voice was gnarled and born from age-old steel dust and wilting promises.

"I'm back!"

16

THE NEWBORN SANGUISA

ichal dropped the stethoscope and backed away from the bed. His fear was pungent. I didn't take my eyes off Draven as he stood up, rolled his head, and hissed. Hot breath like curdled innards went right in my face. I stood firm as I regarded him. He looked like something straight out of *The Night of the Living Dead,* only this deranged creature came with a nice set of lethal fangs. I went to move forward but Sun yanked on my arm and I stumbled back. Draven stretched his neck to sniff out fresh meat. His infrareds settled on Michal.

Holy shit.

Michal was a few feet away and about to become Draven's midnight snack if I didn't do something about it. I pulled my arm free from Sun's grip and called out.

"Draven."

It was enough to grab his attention. His spidery eyes darted between me and Michal. I glanced at Sun.

"Get him out of here now."

She went for Michal as I moved in front of them. Draven looked at me. My skin crawled at his grisly voice.

"Doc made good on his promise." He showed me his palms and laughed. "I'm still alive!"

Yeah. No kidding.

But I would have selected a different word to describe his moldy chowder-like complexion. His now blotchy skin was sallow and sagged in thick tucks at his throat. His hair hung stringy and thin over his scalp.

What have I done?

There was no time to dwell. "You're right, I did say that you wouldn't die tonight, and you didn't."

He gave a throaty chuckle and looked at Sun and Michal as they made a dash toward the lab door. I followed his gaze to see Sun usher Michal forward as she reached for the flaps of the plastic wall. When I glanced back at Draven, he ran his tongue over chaffed lips.

"But you didn't say the same for anyone else here, doc."

I could literally hear the whirl of my pulse a moment before Draven vanished from sight. *Damn.* He moved fast, and in the next moment, he was behind Sun and clawing at her shoulder. I went after him as Sun screeched and tried to shove Michal through the plastic flaps and into the airlock chamber, but Draven flung her across the room before the action could be completed. Michal yelped as he tripped forward and fell on his knees in front of Draven. He scurried across the floor as Draven laughed and moved in on him.

I barely heard the shattering glass and the scientific gadgets crashing all around as Sun landed on the benchtop somewhere behind me. I homed in on Draven who was now within arm's reach. I hurled myself onto his back as he reached for Michal. His leathery neck disappeared into his shoulders as I latched onto him and hooked my claws into his face. He struggled as the stench of his skin overwhelmed me. I dug my fingers into his face as hard as I could and roared. That was when his brute strength locked in. He was a vampire on steroids. I knew I couldn't contain him for long. I gripped his head with one hand and punched hard into his temple to restrain him long enough for Michal to get up and escape the room.

"Piss off, doc!"

Draven's massive knuckles pounded me square in the forehead. *Crack.* My skull almost split in half and at the same time he snarled and started to back up and thrash madly, breaking my flesh like a stinging laceration. I held on tight, locking my nails into his face and repeatedly smashing into his head. It was like pounding into a tenpin bowling ball. I roared again and squeezed my thighs around his torso, hanging on as we were flung backward.

He stilled for a transitory moment as his lofty frame

inflated with a gulp of air before he twisted rapidly and struck my head. *Boom.* My nose snapped and bent with crabbed fingers peeling my skin like bloody floss. My own gore blinded me, and another blow flashed brilliant white behind my eyes. My teeth felt like mulch and my jaw shattered with the next incoming blow. Giddiness took hold as I began to lose my grip on him, barely managing to stop myself from slipping by hooking my fingers into his ear.

Draven growled as I glanced at Michal scrambling to his feet. His eyes bulged as he stood frozen on the spot.

"Go!"

For God's sake, go!

Next thing I knew, my ears were whistling, and I was hurtling toward the other side of the room. It was a fleeting experience, and so was the hard thwack against my face when I slammed into the wall. Everything throbbed. I sprung to my feet and darted for the cot, snapping a hollow steel leg from the bedframe as Sun moved in on Draven who was closing in on Michal. Her fangs glistened as she pushed herself between Michal and Draven, and plunged a shard of glass into Draven's chest.

It was only a second as she spread her arms to barricade Michal, backing away as Draven looked at her. His chest sunk with his wheezy breath.

"You—you stabbed me?"

Michal trembled behind her. I knew the poor sod wasn't game enough to make a move in this moment. I gripped the bed pole and edged toward them, sneaking up behind Draven as he peered down at the jagged glass protruding from his gut.

"Draven?" Sun's voice trembled as she glanced at me. "You're not yourself, we gave you to viral vector, remember?"

Draven shook his head. "I-I don't feel so good."

His corpselike fingers folded over the glass as I gripped the bed pole and crept closer.

"It's just the side effects of the vaccine. It's going to be okay." Sun stepped closer to him. "You just need to relax so that we can fix this, okay?"

Draven looked at Sun and my hairs prickled as he cackled a reply. "It's not going to be okay."

Draven tore the glass from his stomach and in one fluid motion stabbed it into her throat. Blood poured out in a flood. Michal screamed. Sun gurgled and grappled at the shard as she collapsed to the floor. Draven roared and lunged for Michal. I was right behind him, driving the pole through his back.

He let out a loud scream and hunched forward, gripping the pole as it pierced through to the other side of his body. I jammed it further into his back and released a growl of my own. He yanked the pole clean from his body and threw it aside. In the next moment, he was tearing at my torso in a frenzy.

The room sweltered. He turned into a killing machine. I caught the madness reflecting in his eyes and knew we were goners. My body burned as he hissed and slashed at me, shredding my arms. My insides were spilling freely from my gashed body as I tried to grab his heart. But as soon as I lunged my fist into his chest, he gripped my arm and snapped it. *Crunch.* My bones shattered and he held me fast and poised his other clawed hand above my heart. My legs almost buckled as he twisted my broken arm.

"It's too bad that I never got to know you, doc," Draven laughed. "I guess it was all just meant to go to shit."

Avila's face flashed behind my eyes. *Could I leave her behind to face this world alone? Did I have a choice?* Choice felt like the sinkhole of hopelessness that was about to become my chest. He snarled and started to move, and I braced myself for impact when he jerked, a sudden intake of air gushing from his mouth. His eyes widened and blood bubbled from his lips, dribbling down his chin as a shard of glass appeared in his throat.

Huh?

Sun came into view behind Draven. She was a ghoulish platinum demon as she twisted the glass deeper into his flesh. His fingers began to slip from my arm, enabling me to yank myself free as he spluttered and turned toward Sun. He roared and went to fling himself at her but Lena's Amazon-like figure appeared out of nowhere as she planted a roundhouse kick to the side of his head. It was enough to throw him off balance. He staggered, giving me the opportunity to follow up with a few sharp jabs to his gut with my good hand.

His blood drenched his chest as he stumbled backward. Lena and Jamie grabbed a sheet of the plastic wall and folded it around him. He made an unearthly screech and thrashed around before Lena booted his ankles hard and he fell to the ground in a tangle of plastic.

I launched myself on top of his squirming figure, holding him fast and gesturing at the plastic walls. "More! Hurry!"

They ripped plastic sheeting from the walls to secure the super vampire whose struggles lessened as we rolled him within resilient layers of suffocating fabric until he was finally restrained and out cold.

The fight was over, and we had survived. I took gulps of air and looked down at his wrapped body, feeling my own body begin to repair the injuries suffered by the monstrous creature I had created. Illness settled in my stomach as my thoughts collected over what I had just done. It was Lena's thick Latino accent that pulled me back to the present.

"What in the hell is that thing?"

I shrugged. "Draven Sanguisa. Worse than any horror movie."

"Ha. You created the first ever Sanguisa?"

"Seems to be the case."

She glanced around the tattered lab. Equipment, glass,

and blood now replaced the working space we had created. "So, what's the next move?"

"Chains, and lots of them." I gestured at the Sanguisa. "This won't keep him down for long. He will revive and tear through this plastic within a few hours at most. We need to secure him properly so that I can figure out what to do with him."

She nodded. "I know where a bunch of them are stored down in the rail tunnels."

"Take Jamie and Sun and get them. I'll stay here with Michal; and Lena, the next time I tell you not to open a door, please listen. You could've got yourself killed."

She smirked as she started to back away. "So, could've you, *master*."

ILLUSIONARY PROMISES

*N*umbness born of calamity was a footslog pounding against the sidewalk. My head hurt as much as my heart as I stalked the District V streets while the Sanguisa vampire slumbered deep in the subway chutes beneath the city. *Abomination.* Lengths of plastic sheeting choked the air from his body along with the steel chains that wrapped and anchored him to the putrid underground walls. The beast was secure but I couldn't say the same about my current state of mind. Internal warfare trapped me in no-man's-land as I headed to nowhere in particular.

What an idiot. I pushed my hands deep in my pockets and buried my chin in my jacket collar, barely hearing the rain slamming against the dome above as I contemplated how far my desperation to hold onto my daughter boarded on stupidity. Michal had been right when he argued that the viral strain wasn't ready for transfer. Not only had I failed in my attempt to produce a cure before the ceremony, but I had made things a whole lot worse by creating a hellion vampire. Charity was nowhere in sight as I forged ahead, the pressure in my chest radiating like hot stones. I needed time to think my way out of this disaster.

As it was, time was impartial. It was there, lingering like an eternal emptiness. I couldn't turn back the clock to retrieve the last few hours as much as I couldn't alter the days between now and the Claiming Ceremony. Time was a double-edged sword that swallowed my hopes to revive humanity and would devour Avila's.

My girl would be lost to me.

I walked like a madman through the dark streets while the rest of the city remained desolate during the final hours before dawn. I had avoided returning home in District V after leaving the subway. Home felt like a farce that would provide little comfort given the circumstances. I was starkly aware that my real home was as unreachable as hamburgers and sunlight. *Home was wherever Scarla was.* It was her precious soul behind the amber eyes I had once known, and it was everything I had lost to immortality. I halted to press my head on a light pole. The cold steel was oddly pleasant against my forehead as I studied my boots. The light overhead flickered.

Keep your shit together, Jett.

Anxiety was the enemy that would bring me down

faster than any vampire. Only the strong and durable could survive in the new world. I may have royally screwed up, but my kid still needed me around even if I couldn't return her to humanity. I had to keep my big boy pants intact and figure out what to do about the monster vamp before his existence revealed our deception. Sun was right when she mentioned that the discovery-penalty would mean our death.

A series of distant hollering broke through my sordid self-indulgence. I looked up, realizing that I had wandered far beyond the Crypt grounds to venture off the usual city grid, ending up in the section of Norbury city formerly known as public squalor.

The precarious light pole supporting me intersected two dark alleys. I stood amid rundown buildings covered in faded graffiti, decades-long grime and creeping vines, and the sidewalk that stretched along the narrow laneways was filthier than any pavement on the other side of the great wall. It was evident that Marius' refurbishing plans for District V hadn't extended this far in the dome city. I frowned and pushed off the lamp post, scanning the slums and spotting a steel boom gate about midway along the alley. Several unambiguous "No Trespassing" signs plastered the gate.

Interesting.

My curiosity was piqued enough to investigate. If the current post-apocalyptic experience had taught me anything, it was that nothing was off-limits in the new world. Blame it on an acute version of cause and effect. Nowadays, we all knew that certainty had always been an illusion. Still, I kept to the shadows as I prowled the alleyway, gathering momentum as I approached the boom gates before taking the steel structure in one fluid leap. I leaned back on my haunches when I hit the road on the far side of the gate, and my senses were on high alert as I tuned into my surroundings. A whiff of fertilizer strayed from the rear of the deteriorated apartment buildings at the bottom of the alley. I studied the perimeter of the eastern side of the dome city beyond the buildings. I had reached the dome city boundary where the pliable dome material was tethered to the earth with polypropylene woven tubing and layers of barbed wire. The dome wall itself glowed like the moon.

What must this be in the still of a Bloodfaye night?

Voices and laughter mingled with the background sound of rumbling machinery. Something more than my inner torment was rattling the still of the night. I set off again, keeping light-footed and closing in on the foul scent of horse manure and moonshine shenanigans. When I reached the end of the alley, I slowed my pace and slinked into the doorway cranny of an abandoned building to watch the showstopper. It was delivered via the spectacle of a field of crops droning with farming machinery and dozens of people working amid rows of corn, wheat, and other germinating delights beyond the dome wall.

A few floodlights offered synthetic daylight as I gauged the action beyond the parted meshed gates of the dome wall. I could just discern the massive series of barbed fences bordering the other side of the field while Leavings and vampires alike buzzed around the open field performing various tasks such as operating farm machinery, spraying the crops and bunching produce into containers. The entire area was heavily patrolled by a small legion of Mysticus guards and I could see evidence of progressive construction taking place in the surrounds.

I recalled when Avila had mentioned Marius' intentions to implement an agriculture program to provide fresh produce for our Leavings. It seems that I had stumbled upon its whereabouts. Admittedly, I was surprised to see how established this little set-up was. Production was in full swing and thriving but that wasn't what was dominating my interest at this moment. It was the highly secured compound sanctioned just beyond the gate threshold that seized all my attention. My gaze settled on the black bold letter "X" marking the high, iron-meshed wall of the compound. A chill went through me.

District X.

It had to be the place where Marius kept the stolen Leaving children. Devious sprite. It was plain to see that Marius had ensured an impenetrable form of security in and around the fields, and more so for his covert hidden district. The place was a heavy-duty fortress crawling with whip carrying guards, solid fencing and impassable walls. I even noticed the beginnings of a surveillance system being installed atop the walls. The strategically mounted cameras gave it away.

"Oi! You there!"

"We've got a violation!"

My observations were abruptly interrupted. I looked at the group of guards who were patrolling the dome gates as a few of them stopped to sneer at me. *Shit*. I'd been so preoccupied with the scene that I had failed to notice them noticing me. I exhaled slowly as their pallid faces scrutinized the shadows and appeared as brutish as their leather-clad boots stalking the terrain. I began to retreat as about five of the guards started for me.

"Don't move, asshole!"

Yeah, right. I wasn't about to give myself up to this foul-toothed lot. The guards growled and increased their pace to a sprint as I spun around and hot-footed it back down the alley.

"That was an order to stop, vampire!"

"Get him!"

I could sense the blood-hungry adrenaline stoking their energy as their boots stampeded behind me, but I had a good ten-meter head start on my side as I raced down the dark road with my pulse blazing along with my feet. I took the boom gate in a matter of seconds before ducking off the alleyway to cut through the narrow passages offered by the derelict apartment buildings studding the quarter. It wasn't long before the sound of their chase faded behind and I had appeared to have lost them. I emerged from the rundown section of the city minutes later to stroll the rest of the way back to my brownstone complete with yet another compelling revelation.

The new world had again made good on uncertainty and illusionary promises, but I had my own demons to deal with.

BACKFIRE BLUES

*P*lum and pineapple filtered into my senses as I gazed absently at the bouquet of frangipanis taking center stage on Marius' polished dining table. Or was it candy and spices that allured my transitory attention? The flowers had a unique scent and I almost had an urge to squish one of the fleshy white petals while Avila and I waited for *lord arrogance* to join us. We were here to discuss all things Claiming Ceremony and the like. The event would be held in three nights time and I guessed it was important to some. However, my mind was far from bogus vampire ceremonies; I had a bad case of backfire blues and I still needed to figure out what to do with the newborn Sanguisa.

Alive or dead?

That was the choice facing me. We could either keep

working what remained of the cultivated bloods in an attempt to reach a viable solution or cut our losses and kill the kid before he caused more trouble than he was worth. Considering how difficult it was to contain his super-charged kindred strength, the latter option was looking rather appealing right now.

Avila's gentle laugh interrupted my thoughts. She sat across the table from me, reaching to fill a silver goblet with the blood offered in the large crystal decanter between us.

"Remember the scene when Louis discovered Lestat alone in that old house near the end of *Interview with a Vampire*?"

I frowned. "Vaguely."

"He was sitting in the dark, feeding on rats and looking as if he had died a thousand deaths and faced the devil more times than an ogre."

"So?"

"So, you look like Lestat and I'm wondering if it has something to do with why you didn't come home last night."

Hmm …. the things we say without uttering a word.

I forced a smile. "Keep wondering, kiddo. This isn't the time or place."

"It never is…."

She looked beyond me, grinning as Marius entered the room. My spine instantly chilled as I half turned to see him striding across the saloon in flowing black satin and shiny red boots. His expression was just shy of elation as he focused on Avila. I swallowed a groan when he plucked a frangipani and presented it to my daughter.

"For you, my beautiful queen."

She took the stem, bringing the flower to her nose and smiling coyly. "Why, thank you, sir."

I wanted to puke as he stroked her hair and fawned all over her. His voice shucked every nerve.

"In Hindu mythology, the frangipani flower is a symbol of devotion between two people, and Buddhism symbolized them as new life and a renewal of energy."

He paused and cupped a palm beneath her chin. "I couldn't think of a better flower to be present here, with you, today."

"And with you, my love," she murmured as he kissed her.

I cleared my throat and cramped my lips shut when Marius regarded me. He reminded me of a superficial smoothie, and he reeked like insincere slick. *Why could Avila not see this?*

"Jett! How rude of me." His face split with his grin and he reached for another flower, thrusting it toward me in a most elegant fashion. "To the new life!"

Give me a break.

"Yeah, thanks." I took the flower and promptly dropped it on the table next to my goblet. Honestly, I had no patience to endure this quaint meet-and-greet. More so with a new breed of souped-up vampire on my hands. I sighed inwardly. There was no choice but to suck it up for Avila. I preoccupied myself by gulping down my civilized blood-drink as Marius sat next to Avila and began to engage his audience.

"I assume Avila has told you about our plans to move the Claiming Ceremony forward?"

"Yep."

He reached for her hand and gave her his version of a smile that meant something special. My stomach constricted. I went for the crystal decanter to refill my goblet. I needed something to distract me from the strain his voice caused as he continued to speak.

"We may be eternal beings, though time is still precious. Why wait?"

"Indeed. What of me here then?" I laughed. "You want me to arrange a bachelor party? Perhaps take care of the hire cars or look for a wedding planner?"

I ignored Avila's scowl as Marius narrowed his black beacons on me before taking a long sip of blood. He licked his lips and gave a grisly smile.

"If only we could still enjoy wine and its heady effects. We may have cause to loosen you up a little, old man."

"Hey, I'm loose." I held his stare. "But I'd feel a whole lot more liberated if you would return the Leaving children to their parents and let them be."

"Impossible."

"Why? What's so impossible about letting human families be together?"

"Dad—" Avila's voice was cold enough to numb me as I realized that she was on board with this disturbing scheme. The cords in Marius' throat amplified.

"Because those children are pertinent to the future of the clan and that is all I am willing to disclose on the matter at this time."

"You don't trust me?"

"Trust is overrated in the new world. You said so yourself."

"True. Though I assumed that we might be moving into curry favor territory, considering that I am here today."

He laughed. "Only time will reveal the extent of your loyalty, Jett. Until then, my interest in the Leaving children are none of your concern other than the fact that your work is vital to their destiny and that of the clan."

I said nothing and leaned back in my chair, realizing that it was as I had suspected – Marius planned on raising the children to one day transform them into the invincible vampires offered by the elusive AB Positive blood. Without the love of their parents chiseled in their psyche, they would make soulless killing machines.

Marius leaned on the table and pressed his fingertips together. "One of us has to think ahead if the Mysticus is to prevail as the dominant kindred bloodline. This is just the beginning of the new world. We don't know how many other clans exist or what's to come."

I immediately thought about Draven. His strength *was* incredible and who knew what other powers he possessed. It was enough to strike fear into my heart. What was I thinking? To allow such a dangerous creature to remain is a risk I wasn't willing to take. I shuddered at the thought of what might happen if he was to escape his subway confinement. Marius was right, the children were none of my concern when there were more pressing and dire matters to deal with, at least for the moment.

The atmosphere was tense. Marius watched me stiffly. I knew that he meant to pluck the thoughts from my mind as I treated him to a triumphant glare. Avila gave an exaggerated sigh. She shook her head and forced a half-hearted laugh.

"Seriously, we didn't come together today to discuss Mysticus politics; rather to talk about a joyous event which will further solidify and bring a sense of community to the clan." Her features thawed about an inch of my resolve. "Now, we just wanted you to be prepared, Dad."

"For—?"

"For the offering ritual prior to the Claiming hour which will take place at exactly midnight."

"Offering ritual?" I flinched. "As in a sacrifice?"

"A Leaving sacrifice, yes."

"What for?"

Avila's expression darkened. I knew these moments were critical to her. "A ritual is about moving out of our ordinary space and crossing the threshold into something more profound. It makes sense that we perform a sacrificial ritual to demonstrate to all Mysticus members that our union is essential to the evolution of the clan." She paused to ensure that her words caught my attention. "Spilling the blood of an innocent will assure purification to the Claiming."

"Where did you pull that garbage from?" I had to look away from her. "Lestat's personal diary?"

She snorted and went to reply when Marius intervened.

"The life of a Leaving symbolizes longevity and opulence and is to become a tradition in all future Mysticus Claiming Ceremonies." He grinned. "We do have to honor the primitive instincts driving us all from time to time and pay homage to the vampire gods. Livvy and I shall feast on the blood of a Leaving woman prior to the Claiming."

And the shit just keeps piling and piling.

I sunk my talons into my palms and stood up. I had enough of this bullshit. It was all I could do to survive the overwhelming urge to tear this Crypt joint to pieces along with its egotistical overlord.

"Vampires don't have gods." I looked at my daughter who was fast becoming a stranger to me. "Vampires have horrendous, crud-like demon deities who eat gods for breakfast and scour the sludge beneath the city. Would you care to meet one?"

"Ha. Good one, Dad!"

Avila glanced at Marius and they both laughed. That was when I turned away from them, striding from the room with a belly full of curdled blood and a major decision on my shoulders. Avila called out just as I reached the door.

"Dad, are you okay?"

I paused, etching a notch into the timber threshold with my nails as I looked back at them. Avila's stare appeared as vivid as the wallpaper on my old cell, but I barely saw her pale face examining me. Backfire blues pushed my mind into a thousand pieces as I nodded.

"I'm fine."

Just fine.

19

SHIT-FED MONGRELS

The energy in District V was anything other than ordinary and I hated it as much as the walking dead parading along the sidewalk. Fraudulent grins arranged on fake plastic faces made my head spin. My fingers strained over the golf cart steering wheel as I made my way back home. As if it wasn't bad enough that my rejuvenating bones still ached from last night's unexpected fiasco, I was looking down the barrel of a hard choice, but the sickening sight of the festive ornaments made everything that much worse.

Ugh. Someone please shoot me right now.

But a bullet could not take away the vision disturbing me. It was difficult not to notice the silver and gold rattan balls that hung from trees and street posts amid strings of fairy lights and wrought iron vampire glyphs. Marius was fully embracing vampire folklore and traditions, bringing back ancient lore to instill a sense of ancestry and belonging to the clan. It was a smart move, but the entire concept made me feel as if caught in a bastardized version of a fictitious world that I couldn't escape.

As soon as I turned off the main thoroughfare and into the quieter parts of the city, my thoughts returned to the pressing matter at hand – killing Draven Sanguisa before he was discovered by the likes of Marius' crew. I wasn't fooling myself into believing that my background in hematology was enough to save me this time around, nor the fact that I fathered the soon-to-be Mysticus queen.

I had made Avila a promise to always protect her. Granted, she was in sync with her supernatural self and the lifestyle it offered, and she was free of the resentment and hatred responsible for the secret sector I had formed. *Life*. Who would have thought I'd ever be a dead man alive fighting against my own kind or having to decide what to do about a primitive breed of kindred I had created by accident.

I would have no doubts about Avila's ability to survive in the new world without me if it weren't that she was about to become queen and a prime target for power hungry vampires like Zaros. Marius was a calculating fiend at the best of times, but he was smart enough to implement a belief system that promoted a sense of self-control to the clan along with his other more unacceptable visions. It was Zaros and kindreds like him who made for unpredictable enemies.

I sucked in a breath when I copped an eyeful of the devil himself sprawled across the small patch of lawn that constituted my front yard. Zaros. *Terrific.* He appeared like a black leathered reptile lazing beneath the muted dome sun with his arms tucked beneath his head as he lay just shy of the set of stairs that led to my front door. He remained still as I stopped the cart and approached him.

"Zaros." His name bit my tongue.

"Hey doc!" He flashed a grin that reeked like sour lemons.

He stood up and began brushing imaginary grass from his leathers before he gestured toward the brownstone.

"Man, you've got some kind of cool crib going on here. I may have to rethink my own prehistoric flavored dwellings; become more domesticated like you."

"What do you want?"

"Always direct."

"Life's too short not to be."

"Always a comedy show too." He ran a bejeweled hand over his afro. "A shorter life-span can easily be arranged."

"Yeah, no shit." I was expecting Sun and Michal any minute. "Seriously, why the hell are you here, Zaros?"

"Hmm—do I detect a knot in your tightly woven white-boy knickers?" He laughed. "Is there someplace else you need to be other than in the moment with me?"

"Is that a trick question? Let's cut the bullshit; you're here to find out if I'm going to support you in your endeavors to overthrow Marius—" He went to say something but I kept talking. "Ah, yes, and not to forget the nice bonus threat hanging precariously over my head."

"I'd rather call it gentle persuasion."

"What planet are you on? You hit me sideways with threats to kill my daughter when she becomes queen and that's persuasion to you?"

Oddly enough, that sentence sounded rather normal.

"When you put it like that then I can see your point. I heard tell they pushed the Claiming Ceremony ahead."

"And?"

He made a sly gesture which resembled a shrug. "Come on, doc, for a smart guy you can be as dumb as a donkey on heat."

He paused and looked beyond me. My nostrils twitched as the distinct odor of blood fangsta blew my way. I ignored lofty emerald eyes and creature scarecrow as they sidled up next to Zaros.

He sneered. "Means you are going to have to let me know whose side you're on before your kid makes the choice for you."

The goon-vamps laughed, and white fire seared behind my eyes. I pushed it down with a sharp breath and stepped closer to him.

"Your shit-fed mongrels are stinking up my property."

Zaros said nothing but his eyes blazed while his

mongrels hissed at me. I glanced at them before looking back at Zaros.

"Do I look like a shit-fed mongrel to you?"

He stiffened and clenched his fists. Sun and Michal chose this time to appear in the golf cart steered toward the curb. Sun stopped in front of the brownstone and frowned at the scene on my front lawn.

I started to retreat from Zaros and his donkey crew.

"Time to leave, I have *invited* company to receive."

He glanced at Sun as she strutted toward us in her usual mini-skirt and knee-high get-up. The golden bracelets adorning her wrists shone like wine. Michal stayed put in the cart.

Her eyes narrowed as she gripped her hips. "What's going on?" She was all sass and femininity. She glanced between me and Zaros. *God help us*. The combo was alluring.

Zaros grinned at her. "We're all good, baby girl."

"We had better be."

He regarded her for a long moment before looking back at me with a grim expression. "Dumb as a donkey on heat."

The two goon vampires sneered at me as Zaros slinked closer to Sun. She held his gaze as he stroked the side of her jaw with the backs of his fingers. Her thumping heart drummed in my ear. I noticed her bottom lip tremble slightly. In the next moment, he was gone, leaving Sun as still as the dew at dawn.

"What was that all about?" She said.

She had secrets I would never know.

"Vampire power games are all the rage these days, didn't you know?"

She tossed her blond mane. "I wish I didn't know."

"Don't we all."

I gestured for Michal to get out of the cart. He was transfixed by something unfathomable. *Wait till he gets an earful of what's coming next.*

He nodded abruptly and made a move toward us. I glanced at Sun. "Things have changed. We have much to discuss."

"Okay."

I strode up the stairs thinking of sweet unspoken secrets and dewy dawns I'd never know again. I had failed in my quest to restore humanity. Let the world transform with the arrival of the future Blood Legend. I knew what I had to do.

20

BLACK TARGET DOWN

I gripped the machete handle and ignored the dank grit smothering me. The subway tunnel felt as if it was closing in on me. I paused as my eyes adjusted to the darkness broken sporadically by the flickering tube lights edging the ceiling. The faint sound of dripping water echoing along the shafts ignited my senses. I was moving with ghosts and striking irreversible deals with the devil as I moved in on Draven Sanguisa with the intent to kill.

Miscreant.

I felt lower than a slippery eel for all I had caused to befall the kid, but I couldn't immerse myself in the submerged guilt if I was going to make it through to the other side. Sun and Michal had agreed with my decision that he had to die. The alternative carried grim consequences both for our part in his creation, as well as for the clan – the deadly creature was an unpredictable liability we could ill afford to probe.

I opted to go it alone. This was my mess to clean up and there was no way in hell that I would allow Sun anywhere near the Sanguisa vampire even in my presence. I may be supernatural but I was no superman version of vampire. I had barely managed to survive my last encounter with the beast much less protect Sun. I was just glad that he would be somewhat debilitated from two days chained to the wall and sweating in a plastic cocoon.

Get in and get out. After a restless sleep, I had spent the day hamming out the oncoming scene in my head. The cold Japanese steel blade of the machete was sharp enough to slice through the plastic layers constraining the Sanguisa so that I could sever his head without having to break him out. I chose the method of execution for obvious reasons – efficient appeal. Anything to minimize the suffering for all involved. Draven might be a formidable miscreation on my part, but I didn't want to cause him any more pain than necessary.

Admittedly, that might be a tad ambitious on my part. I knew that the Sanguisa would kick my sorry ass all over Bloodfaye if given half the chance. Tonight, the machete was my Holy Grail. I would do what I had to do to snuff him so that I could determine my next moves. The Claiming Ceremony was looming the following night. When I took the final bend leading toward the subway lab, the madhouse flashbacks faded into obscurity as an acute rush of sensory overload hit my psyche. My hackles raised and I slinked back against the wall, peering ahead to where the tunnel narrowed. The lab door was slightly ajar. *What the hell?* The lab should have been secured but the florescent lights blinking through the small gap of the unlatched door proved otherwise. Chills hit me as the smell of unprocessed blood blew downwind. It was tangy, sweet, and crisp; and it was the classic hallmarks of the newly spilled. I tuned into what may lie beyond the door.

Death sounded like silence. I swallowed the moment and steeled myself before lunging for the door. My steps were fluid and purposeful, the machete blade glinting as I stole along the chipped tiled walls until I stopped short of the lab door. I dared not breathe as my eyes darted to the ground to see the blood seeping from beneath the door, slowly filling the cracks in the concrete. The blood flamed glossy, gaudy, and tasteless as it collected dirty steel dust particles. My whole body trembled as I eased the door open and beheld a dazzling pulp. The putrid lab walls were now exposed as the blackened husks they were prior to installing the makeshift inoculation chamber, and offset the chaos of scientific equipment and gadgets, stools and glass shards reminiscent of the Sanguisa creation. Everything was the same but for the Sanguisa himself where we had left him chained to the wall in a deep roll of plastic which now was strewn in pieces on the ground, the thick chains cast aside. Now fragmented parts of human anatomy lay in a sea of blood.

The Sanguisa was gone. I copped an eyeful of the vertebrae, stripped of muscle, and the tenderly deep pink sequence of a spine laying across the bench amid expelled innards. Blood infused red meat, spilled gore and discharged coils of rust-colored intestines. The ghastly image flashed to the beat of the flickering lights. *Blink.* A decapitated head, unrecognizable. *Blink.* One hollow eye socket, the other gleaming at me. *Blink.* A mouth cracked wide open, frozen in an endless scream.

Blink.

I scanned the room with my eyes but detected no movement. Whoever was responsible for this carnage appeared to be gone. My fingers tightened over the machete handle as I slowly crossed the threshold, pausing to choke back the urge to gag when the bitter odor of guts overcame me. My ears pricked at the sound of a raspy breath and my gaze darted toward the slight sound emanating from where the cot stood broken along the far wall, thin mattress askew. I gasped as I recognized Lena's peroxide-stained hair showing from beneath the mattress.

"Lena."

Her name clung to my lips as I rushed toward her, and the sound of the blinking lights clicked against my nerves as I threw the mattress aside and kneeled on the floor next to her. I flinched and almost recoiled when I saw that half of her face was a raw lump of meat without a trace of skin, one eye like liquefied roe. The flesh on her throat was exposed with bits of flesh pulled off, a splintered hole revealing her larynx as a mess of cartilage and veins. *No!* I opened my mouth to speak but I couldn't find words as the machete slipped from my hand and I reached to cradle her head, trembling when a piece of her scalp, stained with matted scarlet hair, flapped back. The rest of her body was perfect as she lay corpselike in a pool of her lukewarm blood. *Dead.* I had been too late.

"What have you done?" I said the words aloud but I wasn't sure if they were meant for me or her. Why was she even in here? "I—I'm so sorry, Lena."

I was unable to look away from her as I realized that the dismembered body was Jamie, Lena's friend and Shadow Guardian wingman. I exhaled as Lena's blood soaked through my pants while a mixture of fear, grief and repugnance took hold. Only a starved and primitively mutated vampire could do something this heinous to his prey. The Sanguisa. But where was he now?

So much for getting in and getting out. I had a dead friend and a psychotic new breed of vampire on the run who I needed to find and deal with before someone else did; preferably before a repeat of this scene had time to unfold. I went to stand up but froze when a barbed voice came from above.

"Sorry won't undo all that *you've* done, doctor crazy."

My blood went colder than usual as I looked up and scanned the ceiling, spying the Sanguisa' crabbed figure suspended and clinging to the notches above me. His neck twisted and appeared disjointed as his beaded eyes hunted me down and flashed crimson. Blood-tinged saliva foamed at his lips with his hiss.

Chingar.

The backsliding creature was here all along. He could burn with the old railway coal for all I cared. I met his stare and barely heard myself speak over the body rush. "Nice party trick."

"Thanks to you. Did you come here to kill me?"

I went to say something, but I blanked out as the sound of his laughter burrowed deep in my mind before he released himself from the notches to land gracefully on his feet near me. He snarled and I sprang for the machete that still lay on the ground next to Lena. I grabbed the handle but it was knocked back onto the concrete as the base of my skull caved in like a whoopie cushion.

Crack!

I fell forward over Lena and saw stars. Sanguisa launched himself on top of me and broke into a frenzied attack, tearing up my back with scalpel-like talons while he roared as my face jammed into Lena's open throat.

Boom!

The air was gone from my lungs as sanguine fluid, mashed up arteries and the like filled every crevice of my face. It was warm and gooey, but that was the last thing on my mind as the beast saddled me, screeching as he forced his fist through the flesh on my back. I gave a demented groan as he withdrew his palm, taking fistfuls of my bits with him. He beat me senseless as I braced myself against the relentless onslaught. My body became like iron as I homed in on my supernatural strength, summoning the violence in me.

Black.

I felt voltaic and raw as the Sanguisa screeched and tore at my shirt, peeling the skin on my back as I pulled my face from Lena's throat and growled loudly, with saliva trailing down my chin. I blacked out fear and fury as I embodied the knave, the *enfant terrible*. I screamed and moved like a bullet, repeatedly striking my elbows into the Sanguisa's chest before flinging him off me. I grabbed the machete and leapt to my feet, spinning to face him with the blade outstretched as he charged at me.

Black breath.

The steel went into his gut as if slicing through butter. His face contorted as he halted. A static moment and resounding heartbeat. *Ba-boom. Ba-boom.* My brain fizzled as he wrapped his claw-like fingers along the steel, grinning.

"You want me dead but I'm a nightmare you can't kill."

"We'll see about that."

Those were tough words, but they were meaningless and we both knew it despite following up with a hiss as I gripped down on the machete handle. Just as I was about to twist the blade further into him, he slid his torso along the edge of the knife. My boots skidded on gore as I started to back away. He menaced me with a deep growl before thrusting himself forward. The next thing I knew was the pressure of his fingers hooking into my flesh and the sensation of his fangs sinking into my throat, squeezing the blood from my veins. I tried to move but my legs started to give way as my vision tunneled and dizziness took hold. *Freefall.* My blood whooshed right out of me and my thoughts evaporated along with my energy; I was putty in his hands until I was gaunt and bloodless.

His ugly face was a convoluted picture as he withdrew and laughed. The last thing I heard was the snap of my neck before the room stopped blinking.

Black target down.

THE OTHER SIDE

*V*iolet flames rose in the distance over a body of water that resembled a transparent blue gemstone. I stood overlooking a pristine beach, gazing ahead and feeling weightless. The smell of sea salt purified me. I lifted my chin toward the sky, inviting a renewed feeling of vitality as it surged through me. It was different here. Nothing made sense but everything was perfect. I had a strange sense that I could embody any version of myself that I wanted. It was an inner knowing that was as deep as marrow and forgotten in the next moment as I focused on the simulated stratosphere burning an amethyst wildfire. A sense of peace permeated.

Where am I?

"You're on the other side, Jett."

"Huh?"

A bearded man appeared beside me to pluck the thoughts from my mind. He radiated a warm smile and wore a string of scarlet beads over a loose white shirt. His long brown hair fell in waves and glowed with the magenta aura. He looked familiar.

"Jesus?"

"Hell, no. My hair is so much better than Jesus." He laughed and offered me his palm. "The name's Alvin."

"Alvin ....?" My voice trailed as we shook hands and the penny dropped. "You're the all-powerful and elusive witch dude of Sweetwater Valley."

"Not so elusive now, huh?"

Guess not. Though I had no idea why he was the one to greet me here, the place he dubbed as the other side.

"We are strangers, you and me."

All I knew of Alvin was that Clio had sought his help when we needed to create a spell to cloak Shana, the half-bred wolf-baby. Marius had wanted her dead, but I had learned that her survival was vital as she carried the origins of the Blood Legend genes that needed to mature through the generations to produce "the one". Alvin began to loop his beads around nimble fingers. His silvery whiskers twitched.

"I wouldn't be taking time out from Eden's garden for a stranger, and F-Y-I: call me a sorcerer, an alchemist or even a conjurer if you must – but don't call me a 'witch dude'."

Okay. Witch dude has a sore spot.

"It's more of a preference." He shrugged. "The years have made me somewhat particular."

"I get it." A sense of mild frustration shimmered as I realized each of my thoughts were for the taking. I flicked my chin toward the dynamic horizon. "The years have made me dead for good this time, I can feel it."

"Perhaps you're right. Your body *is* currently a bloodless bag of bones lying in human guts and numbles on a filthy subway floor in the city of vampires."

"Thanks for the explicit recount."

"You're quite welcome."

"Are you dead, too?"

He shook his head. "Witch dude, remember?"

A bizarre feeling of euphoria flooded me as I watched him twist the beads around his fingers before releasing them to then repeat the process in the opposite direction. If this was death, it wasn't so bad. At least the pain was gone. "So, let me guess, you are here to escort me to the Pearly Gates or something?"

He laughed. "Nah. Clio sent me. I came here to remind you."

"Of what?"

He gestured toward the sea that moved to an ethereal tide. "In about thirty seconds, the greatest love of your life will appear to escort you to the hereafter if you so wish to join her."

"I have a choice, then?"

"We always have a choice."

A series of fragmented memories flashed into form as I peered toward where the grainy sand met the sea below a display of lights more vivid than the Aurora Borealis. I felt as if all my pieces were finally merging into completeness. As if there was nothing more left to do.

"Ah, but there is much more left for you, Jett," Alvin said. "That's why I'm here remember?"

I barely heard him as Scarla arose from nowhere to appear on the shoreline some few hundred meters from us. She wore a sheer white dress and rows of auric bracelets adorned her wrists. I couldn't hear her, but she laughed as she followed prints along the sand and toyed with the waves lapping at her feet. Her wild hair caught the breeze and cascaded like golden silk down her back. *Angel.* My soul lady was here for me.

"I'm going home."

"It's an option."

I kept my eyes trained on Scarla. She was the woman who had arrived in my life years before the apocalypse to steal my heart only to be brutally taken from me at the hands of a ginger bearded hawker. She was all that I had wanted in this world and I had been lost without her. I felt the familiar yearning swell in my soul when she turned to smile at me.

"It's an option that I want."

"Understood." Alvin thumbed his wiry whiskers. "I too have loved, but never have I been so fortunate to have shared such a deep connection with another the likes of which the two of you share."

I didn't look at him. "She showed me what it meant to really open my heart to pure love. She showed me who I was and the type of person I could be."

"The type of person who wouldn't turn his back on his true purpose to assist those in need—."

"No one needs me now. Avila is giving herself to Marius. She will never be the girl I raised after this. He will take every ounce of what's left of her humanity and empathy before long."

"You're wrong, Jett. The world has transformed with dark energy and now, more than ever, it needs those among the living who are pure in heart to keep the balance until the true Blood Legend arrives. You are still needed to play out your role in Avila's life, as well as for the greater good of humanity. Your daughter has a special secret."

"Riddles. You've been talking to Melissa."

"There are no riddles in truth. Melissa's messages were your cues to decipher and follow at will. Even in our higher-state positions, we are not permitted to hand you the information on a silver platter—. It must be given enough to help guide or warn. It's not how it works on this side."

"Like I said, riddles."

I was distracted when I noticed Scarla pushing strands of

hair from her face and her dress clinging to her thighs as she started walking toward us. *Home.* Her energy expanded like an unfurling petal to connect with mine. I smiled. She felt more ardent and beautiful than any star in the universe and my heart almost burst with the love encapsulating me. I wanted to run to her, but Alvin's words bound me to the spot.

"Your presence on earth is vital to the unfolding Blood Legend legacy. The girl of tomorrow with the unique bloodline will need you to help her embrace and understand her greater purpose someday." He gestured toward Scarla. "You know that love is a powerful force. You can feel that truth deep in your soul, yes?"

"Yes."

"Then you will know that the love between you and your soul lady is a rare gift strong enough to last and flourish over time and space if you honor it. She will always be with you, Jett."

Illusions?

"No illusions, only truth. Allow the truth of what I say to seep into and affect you. *Then you will know, my friend.*"

He didn't say those last words out loud, but I heard them regardless. I frowned and looked at Scarla who was approaching ever closer. To reclaim and rebuild a home from yesterday. A sense of urgency formed at my spine and split my thoughts. I *needed* to be with her yet something powerful pulled me in the opposite direction as the desperate sound of my name called from another dimension.

"Jett! Stay with me, Jett, please!" A heart-wrenching sob stifled along an invisible barrier separating realms. I recognized the voice as Sun's. "Jett, don't go. You can't just leave me here in this world without you!"

"Sun?"

Alvin gave me a critical look. "It's time to choose now."

"Yes."

My pulse quickened as I beheld the violet lights blazing across the sky, deadlocking me with an impossible choice that I couldn't escape. *Scarla.* She halted midway between the space separating us. Her teeth grazed her bottom lip as amber eyes caught me in an intimate flame made for two. Her voice penetrated my soul like a gentle caress:

"I know it burns and that the distance between us hurts, my love. I miss you so much and love you even more. But your home is always inside of you, Jett. You take our love with you in your heart and soul. Our work together transcends through time and space, I'll always be here, with you."

"I love you."

"I know." Her smile was honey as she waved, and my insides screamed when her final words fell into my mind. *"Waiting for the day—."*

"Waiting for the day."

Her image began to fade and the constant dull ache her death had left behind returned as she disappeared from view. My neck started to throb like crazy and my mind whirled. I gulped air and spluttered as Sun's face doubled in my vision and the subway lab flashed into my awareness.

Blink.

"Jett! Thank God!"

Blink.

Sun threw her arms around me and I flinched. My throat felt like sandpaper as she thrust her wrist at my lips, offering me her vein. "Drink."

Blink.

It was all I could do as remnants of the other side and the feeling of Scarla's energy faded into reality and blood-soaked carnage, and the knowledge that a fierce vampire called Sanguisa was now on the run.

"Welcome back. I'd thought you were gone for good," Sun said.

I almost was.

"It is a curious thing, the death of a loved one. We all know that our time in this world is limited, and that eventually all of us will end up underneath some sheet, never to wake up. And yet it is always a surprise when it happens to someone we know. It is like walking up the stairs to your bedroom in the dark, and thinking there is one more stair than there is. Your foot falls down, through the air, and there is a sickly moment of dark surprise as you try and readjust the way you thought of things."

— Lemony Snicket

THE CLAIMING

Sun pushed a thin, light rod into my palm as we stood on the sidelines of the Crypt courtyard. Pre-Claiming ceremony celebrations were in full swing. My feet felt tethered to the earth as I dealt with the hyped crowd and music. I strained to hear.

"It was my grandmother's. I think you could use it more than me tonight," Sun said.

I looked at the slim stave. It was about the length of my palm and crafted from rose quartz with a silver finish at the tip. A small chunk of raw crystal was mounted in delicate silver claws at its head.

"So—I'm going to use this to slay the enemy?"

"If only it were that easy." She folded my fingers over the stave and gave a half laugh. "It's a crystal energy wand. It's not much, but it might help you from going over the edge tonight. My grandmother believed in it."

"Do you?"

Her eyes glazed. "I believed in her."

I slipped the wand into my pocket. I didn't have the heart to tell Sun that it was a hopeless cause. A crystal energy wand was cute, but it wasn't going to fix the fact that I had royally screwed up. Lena was dead and there was a ruthless Sanguisa in the wild who ate vampires for breakfast.

Archfiend.

The definition of diabolically evil had gone lower than the empty pit in my stomach. I shuddered and tuned out to my surroundings. The feeling of Sanguisa fangs sinking into me and siphoning my blood was fresh enough to shoot daggers in my nerves. He had been long gone by the time I returned from the other side. The Sanguisa's whereabouts was a mystery but that wasn't the only sickening part. It was his calculated savagery that made me nauseous. I knew that I couldn't bring him down alone. Of course, that cheery prospect would have to get in line as I faced an even brighter failure – Avila's doomsday ceremony.

I flinched when Sun reached for my shoulder. The impetuous sound of drums beating against the rowdy crowd blasted me back to reality. It was quite unfortunate.

"Jett?"

"Huh?"

"The offering." She gestured toward the stage. "I think it's about to begin."

It took all I had to keep it together as I focused on the hedonistic vampires clustering on the courtyard lawn. Fanged men and women frisked to the hypnotic beat of the drums. Hisses, mixed with the lingering scent of blood and rose oil, saturated the air with seduction. An array of retro-style threads created a colorful patchwork audience that shone as bright as their hair beneath the glowing lanterns and strings of fairy lights dangling above the courtyard.

I looked up. The dome illuminated white silver, reflecting the rising full moon denied to us on this side of the egg. I was part of an entombed burlesque saga. I was caught in a twisted version of *Queen of the Damned,* only my daughter was the one about to pledge to hell and damnation. This was life imitating art at its most sardonic. I tore my eyes from the mob and saw the stage. Things did not improve.

Smoking hot succubus.

The stage was scorched with fire and women. Dark goddesses danced among the flames offered by burning candelabras pulsing to the hypnotic beats produced by the drummers behind them. Their barely clad bodies gleamed like smooth velvet masked with smoke, rose embellished wrought iron and the dainty silver chains on their hips. They were intoxicating but their beauty was lost on me, despite the lashings of sheer fabric accentuating their femininity. The entire affair was flagrantly romantic, somewhat perverted, and loathsome. No wonder my head ached.

Sun's voice was the comfort I couldn't quite grasp. "What a circus."

I stared ahead. "The circus I couldn't prevent."

Her skin felt cold yet soft when she clasped my chin to command my attention. "Maybe you weren't meant to prevent it, Jett. Maybe you were just supposed to be there for the people you care about as we all adjust to the new life."

Her gilded eyes found my soul and I started to quiver on the inside. "Maybe you just had to find a way to accept what you cannot change."

Ouch.

She had a way of stirring deep truths but her honest perspective could not remove my mistakes nor could it fix them. The Sanguisa flashed through my mind. Being there for the people I loved did not equate to unleashing a demonic force on them. I was about to voice as much when the drumming stopped and the crowd hushed. The sound of Marius' silvery tones congealed in my veins.

"Welcome!"

He walked on stage sheathed in shiny white leather and chunky black boots. His jet hair slicked to his scalp like licorice. The vamp partygoers clapped as the on-stage dancers flocked to him, and he patted their behinds one by one as they each gave him a kiss before vanishing from the stage. His dark gaze lingered over the last sultry blond as she sashayed from view before he cast a smile at the audience.

"Mysticus vampires, greetings and welcome to the clan's first ever Claiming Ceremony!"

A round of applause accompanied a few melodious responses.

"Marius, I love you!"

"Hell yeah, baby!"

Laughter.

"Bring on the ascension!"

There was a loud ovation.

"Where's our vampire queen?"

Marius laughed. "Oh, I see you lot are as eager to get on with the ceremony as much as me. How very exciting! All of you are about to witness a crucial event that will be recorded along the vampiric timeline as an evolution of vampirism. You've got to realize that there is great power in love and connection, and that, my friends, will lead us toward ascension. Who knows what treasures lie in our future! It's a good time to be undead!"

Another generous helping of applause and exuberant praise ensued. I tuned out to the noise of the crowd and focused on the man who aroused hatred in me like no other. The blame consumed me. He was responsible for forcing my family into an irreversible life of death and now he was about to take the final victory – everything good still left in my girl. I didn't know how being around for that was going to do me or her any good.

I fingered Sun's wand in my pocket as Marius greedily lapped up the adoration lavished upon him by his minions, laughing and working the crowd like a pro. The man was in his element. It was clear that he was born to be a vampire overlord. I felt dirty on the inside just watching him. I knew that his devotion to darkness and his conniving manner would always be our greatest discrepancy. He laughed some more and hushed the mob.

"Ladies and gentlemen, shall we have ourselves a vampire Claiming Ceremony?"

"Yes!"

"Are you ready to greet your new queen?"

"Yeah!"

"Bring her out!"

Marius poked a finger at the audience.

"Who's as love-hungry as me?"

His final words sent the crowd wild. A sea of arms rose and shook as the horde shouted their approval. The energy peaked when one woman leapt onto the stage, skillfully landing next to Marius. She ripped open her flimsy silver tank top revealing salmon nipples on opaline skin that saluted the whistling audience. Her fangs glinted through the yellow hair clinging to her face as she flung herself at him.

"Take *me* as your queen, master!"

Marius flinched.

"Easy there, Lamia," he said as he pried her talons from his arms.

The crowd heckled, tootled and booed as two beefy guards appeared from nowhere to seize the rogue vampire. Their expressions remained stony as they gripped her arms.

Marius smirked. "Be a good vampire and run along now, darlin'."

The woman spat and cursed at the guards as they dragged her away. The crowd cackled louder as she issued a drawn-out hiss before she disappeared off stage.

Marius gave a dismissive wave. "It appears as though some of us are just a bit more love *ka-razy* than others. Alas, we all know that my heart belongs to one woman only – here she is, Lady Avila!"

Disintegration.

Everything inside me shattered as Avila appeared from between the curtains at the side of the stage. Her long dark locks contrasted against her pearly white dress that revealed too much for my liking, and her wrists shimmied with rows of silver bangles that matched the delicate crystal headpiece suspended on her crown. She paused briefly, scanning the audience with a wave before walking into Marius' embrace. A series of whistles and catcalls followed until she gave a coy smile and addressed her devout subjects.

"Hello my fellow Mysticus creatures! Your fervent greeting flatters me. I am supremely honored, and I thank you for being here with us tonight to commemorate our union. As your queen, I vow to always support and stand by your king—even when he gets too much to handle!" She stopped to laugh. "Seriously though, through our love and devotion to one another and to you, it will be my pleasure to help guide the Mysticus clan toward a prosperous and powerful tomorrow!"

Applause erupted along with a string of idolized praise.

"Simply stunning."

"Dark beauty. I know why she stole his heart."

"She just owns that dress!"

Please! I swallowed a snort and briefly contemplated leaving. Surely, Avila wouldn't miss my presence here. I could hardly stomach any more of this ghastly scene. Sun shot me a look and I groaned inwardly. I knew she sensed my inner turbulence. I went for the wand in my pocket and prayed for the balance she said it would produce. My fingers tingled. It was torturous to be here, but I couldn't leave Avila until the deed was done and she was safely tucked away in the Crypt. Her presence on stage made her vulnerable. That much I knew even as Marius prepared to initiate the ceremony.

My eyes rested on my girl as he took her hand. She looked giddy. Her milky complexion flushed under the subdued lighting and her lips were swollen scarlet. The girl who spoke wonder in my heart from the moment she was born looked happier than I had ever seen her. *My little nugget.* Perhaps Sun was right in that my role here was meant to support my loved ones in their choices instead of resisting them. Marius' voice rose over the courtyard to interrupt my introspective moment.

"Ladies and gentlemen, the Claiming hour is almost upon us. I urge you to practice your stealthy gifts of honorable silence as our chosen Leaving woman joins us for the offering ritual."

A collective gasp hung in the air before quiet befell the throng. The drummers began a gentle tempo as Marius gave a discreet nod toward an obscured figure lurking in the shadows at the left of the stage. All eyes followed his unspoken cues as the curtains slowly parted. I exhaled, mentally preparing myself for the sight of a terrified human who was about to face her death but the sonorous tongue of Zaros struck cold in my heart instead.

"Surprise!" His brawny figure was a swathe of black leather striking against flashing onyx eyes as he paused at the curtains to plant his feet wide and grin at Marius.

"What? Not who you were expecting to see?"

"Hoped, more like it."

Zaros laughed before he flicked a bejeweled hand toward the back of the courtyard and strode onto the stage with the slick of a preternatural hunter. My senses were instantly on high alert as I went to move closer to Avila, weaving through knitted bodies and making my way toward the front of the stage. Sun stuck close behind me as the crowd gasped and huffed before a sudden screech sounded from the back of the courtyard. I turned around to see the crowd whirling and clustering together as a series of screams emanated from the rear.

"What's happening?"

"Argh – they're demons!"

"Wh-what is that thing?"

More ear-piercing screams and dreadful hissing chilled me to the bone as I tried to decipher the situation. Something terrible was going on at the rear of the courtyard but I couldn't see from my mosh pit position. Avila shrieked and Sun grabbed my arm. I looked at my daughter as the stage curtains flung open and about a dozen of Zaros' crew strode into view. They were armored in patchy brown leather and clutched wooden stakes but my attention was drawn to the creature who slinked alongside them – Draven Sanguisa.

Shit.

Marius' guards rushed onto the stage. Zaros and his crew stopped short of Marius and Avila, but my vision homed in on the Sanguisa who was now prowling the edge of the podium, growling and hissing at the audience. I didn't hear his gnarly laughter or the terrified gasps, nor did I notice the hysterical cries echoing in the night. Death had come calling. My miscreation had multiplied. I knew it even before Zaros' opened his mouth to impart what I most feared.

"Now that I have your full attention, I would like to introduce Bloodfaye's newest members who will assist me as your true overlord toward the ascension Marius here likes to shamelessly dangle in your face."

He paused and smiled, and that was when I glimpsed the Sanguisa stalking either side of the courtyard perimeter. I spotted four in total and they were accompanied by more members of Zaros' crew. Their deathlike features stole my breath to the point that I barely heard Zaros speak again.

"It is indeed a good time to be undead. Ladies and gentlemen, meet the Sanguisa!"

Panic rippled like a silent wave. Mine was an internal scream.

23

QUEEN AVILA

arius' eyes bulged. He gripped Avila's
hand as Zaros stood like a vainglorious
cock penetrating the crowd with his dark stare. The stage
was brimming with white-leather muscle and dingy stake-
carrying crew who sneered at one another. However, my
eyes were trained on my girl who was stranded amid the
macabre brew. The atmosphere hung rigid on the sounds
of prowling Sanguisa and their hideous hissing as they
harassed the crowd fringing the courtyard. I stole between
the vampires who bunched at the foot of the stage.

Atrocious.

Now that Zaros had a dirty trump card to play, he was
obviously here to use it to overthrow Marius in his quest
for power. How he had happened upon and managed to
tame the Sanguisa was a mystery. Even more astounding
was how he discovered his ability to turn others like him.

There was no time to dwell on the expositions. The tension in the courtyard was mounting and a sense of foreboding threatened. Zaros laughed as he stalked across the stage to where the Sanguisa stood at the ledge of the far corner glaring at the audience. Zaros threw an arm around the beast and smirked.

"Now, before we get into the nitty-gritty of why I've crashed this fancy shindig, let me reassure you of your safety. I may look like a terrible vampire, but I do have heart." He fisted his chest. "The Sanguisa, on the other hand, are every bit of the blood-craving bogeymen they appear to be. Any dodgy move will set them off. Believe me, you want to avoid risking their very unpleasant qualities."

"Hells bells and evil spells."

"Disturbing—h-how is this so?"

The crowd broke into a tumult of shrieks while the Sanguisa on stage threw open his arms and chortled. His dark stringy hair stuck to his scalp as he proceeded to bow. His spidery eyes darted as Zaros stepped back as if to give him the floor. As the commotion unfolded, I continued to slip between the last of those who occupied the space separating me and the stage.

"What just happened? Where's our blood-show?"

"What is that creature?"

"I don't—"

One woman clutched her heart.

"I-I can't look away. He's utterly repulsive!"

I stopped short of the stage. Avila was only meters from me. The jittery crowd pushed around me but she immediately saw me. Her slight figure was almost ingested by the burly guards surrounding her. She looked at me and shook her head. I knew she meant for me to stay put and I would for as long as bloodshed remained at bay. Besides, I was all too familiar of how Sanguisa responded to sudden moves. My blood rushed as Marius released her hand, shifting away from the grouped guards. His voice was thunderous.

"Threats, Zaros? You must be forgetting yourself. Allow me to remind you of your place by issuing a warning. Take your punk-villain freak show and get the fuck off my stage before I have you ass-whipped from here to China."

He swished a hand through the air, cuing his guards for action. "That isn't a request."

"Ha!"

White-leathered Mysticus guards went to move but were instantly sidestepped by Zaros' men. They exchanged a series of snarls as they showed their teeth, flexed muscle and assessed one another. I recognized Zaros' usual vermin accomplices in *emerald eyes* and *scarecrow* but they were the least of my concerns as the threat of violence fumed. A few of the guards nudged and thumped chests as they began to slowly circle the stage, moving between flaming candelabras and rose-studded twisted iron. With Avila's henchmen and adversaries playing hangman appetizer, she was free to move. Her gaze flitted to me and she bit her lip as I motioned her over to me. She started to edge closer, halting when Zaros gave a biting laugh.

"Requests, requests! If only I had a dime for every bid you ever ordered, sir."

He flailed his arms while the Sanguisa menaced beside him. "Oops, that's right—dimes are worthless in the new world where only blood and violence speak on the devil's tongue. Mysticus members, are you not as sick and tired of Marius' constant demands as much as me?"

A restless murmur spread among the people, but he talked over them. "Listen up vamps, I am here to present to you an alternative way of life. Marius never gave you a choice but that's about to change."

What a crock.

These guys were the definition of crazy comics, albeit dangerous ones. It was obvious that Marius was fighting a blowing gasket. His face was flushed red as he strutted like a mosquito bitten swindler out for blood.

"Outrageous! How dare you challenge my authority. My visions and actions have manifested Bloodfaye – the sanctuary *you* call home. It was I who created the dome city and, in the process, provided the security and freedom for us all as we move into a more empowered and civilized existence as we embrace our supernatural gifts together, for better or worse."

"I choose worse." Zaros smirked. "See what I'm

saying? This guy's head is too far up his pompous ass to notice how *you* really feel."

The crowd's laugher bordered on hysterics, and bewilderment set in as Marius growled and the Sanguisa stalking the courtyard perimeters moved toward the front of the courtyard, closer to the stage. It was the unchecked gasps that arose from the people as they passed that revealed their whereabouts. I met Avila's stare. She inched a little closer as Marius' laugher stripped my nerves.

"Weak-minded fool. Do you really think your small posse of rabid vampires are enough to overthrow me? Where did you find them? Copulating with turds in the Norbury city sewer?" He jeered. "I have a legion of loyal guards and the most gifted Leaving scientist to remain in the world behind me to outwit any malformed vampire species you could ever conjure."

"Are you certain of that, home-boy?"

The stage curtains parted, and it took a few seconds for me to recognize Michal as he walked onto the podium. He was dressed in black leather, carried a wooden stake and his eyes gleamed like apache tears minus the usual spectacles he wore. His pasty complexion rested on contempt as he scrutinized Marius.

Hell, no. I did a triple take. *What did the schmuck do now?*

My eyes were glued on my friend even as the audience started spitting and hissing.

"You wouldn't happen to be talking about my main vamp-man here, Michal, would ya? Turns out, he was recently sired to me which means you are shit out of luck in the super-smarts scientist arena."

Marius's expression darkened as Zaros laughed and proceeded to deliver his proposition to the Mysticus crowd. His afro flickered violet in the light as he paraded the stage.

"With me as your overlord, I promise to give you and our Leavings the freedom to be who you are, follow your deepest desires and live your most fulfilling lives without the fascism and slavery offered by Marius. Would you not prefer the new world to be liberated from tyranny-flavored dictatorship and undemocratic rule? Would you not enjoy a society independent from the suppression and terror the likes of which Marius has shown us?"

"Enough!" Marius roared. His mouth contorted as he rose an arm to signal his guards to act. The bicker-barge show was over. Fangs were exposed to issue snarls. Talons flared at the ready as the corpse contingency party obliged their master's order.

My eyes flew to Avila as the guards began to go at it. Undead on undead. My heart imploded along with my ears. Leather and stakes. Bloodcurdling screams, and the other Sanguisa screeched as they pounced, shredding the violent mash-up of flesh ripping supernaturals.

"Dad!"

"Avila!"

My voice was swallowed by the horde on the lawn as the energy ignited to an uproar and they transformed into cats on hot bricks. Vicious hissing mingled with heated snarls as they started to flay, claw and thrash. *Jab*. A set of razored claws stabbed my back as the weight of a hundred bodies converged on me. I ground my teeth as anger overtook my body. The crowd pushed forward. It was death pit alley, and I was entangled. The ground disappeared from beneath my feet and unearthly Sanguisa roars rose above the chaos. I looked up to see Avila sprinting toward me.

"Dad!"

Avila!

I couldn't form her name for lack of air. My lungs caved as I shoved away the vampire hissing in my face before thrusting a fist into another mongrel who was shoulder-jamming me. The stage landscape blurred with head-to-head clashing. The distinct sound of crunching muscle and snapping bones impaled the courtyard. Zaros barked a command and Draven Sanguisa gave a horrendous growl before charging for my girl. He moved like tomorrow.

"Avila!"

I barged into the guy in front of me in desperation to attain the edge of the stage as her screams echoed in my brain. In seconds, the Sanguisa shadowed the space between us. Rawhide talons expanded from his decayed hands as he rolled his head and howled. Everything faded into oblivion as Avila trembled and stepped back. The Sanguisa sneered and hunched his shoulders before he charged at her. I screamed wildly in an attempt to snare his attention.

"Oi! You – Draven Sanguisa!"

The beast ignored me. I dug my talons into the timber stage and my feet found the ground. I steadied myself against the untamed crowd and was about to propel myself onto the podium when the Sanguisa halted to sniff out the air, moving his neck like a rapacious wolf. Something dramatic shifted and I froze as every supernatural being in the courtyard suspended hostility, watching as the great demon vampire folded to his knees and bowed before Avila.

Silence.

Avila's gaze flew to me and she gave a half laugh. I tried to collect my jaw as the four other Sanguisa slinked across the stage to pay homage to my girl, each of them dropping to their knees. Draven Sanguisa then spoke the words that blew my mind.

"The Sanguisa are here to serve you, Queen Avila."

2 4

THE SECRET

The moments were surreal. Everything slowed down yet played out over a matter of seconds. I blinked rapidly as I watched the strange scene unfold on stage. *Queen Avila?* She stood with the grace of a lady and childlike candor. Her stare grazed over mine, but I was nothing but a patchy depiction of war-torn horror and astonishment as fragments of truth hit me. *Secrets and murder.* Clarity was a series of unbroken signals in my mind and I could barely breathe as memories collected over several days, weeks and even years became transparent, and a long-gone voice revisited.

"She's got a secret, Jett."

"Melissa."

Her name was barely a whisper on my tongue. *Secret genetic codes.* Dreamtime messages encrypted from a mother who dedicated her life's work to biomedical genetic exploration. She had worked for the same underground government agency as Michal, and during the period when they were conducting experiments on Shane's blood no less. Shane was the original Lygarou wolf whose genetics held the primordial werewolf secrets derived from sorcery. *How could I have missed this?* I exhaled slowly as I thought of the plaster on Avila's arm and a wolf called Shana.

"There are no accidents, Jett."

Bittersweet revelation found me and at once I knew that Melissa's death was no accident. She must have uncovered a genetic code in the Lygarou blood at the agency. The vital link to the cure they had wanted to keep under strict lock and key. So much so that they had her murdered. It was the same agency whose quest to transmute original Lygarou blood into a powerful biological weapon eventually infected the world with the V-virus. Those covert dirty experiments on Shane's blood were responsible for millions of deaths and the apocalypse.

The entire courtyard seemed as if entranced by the peculiar turn of events. All remained still but for Marius as he cleared his throat before walking to Avila. He spoke to her softly as my internal world exploded with the final piece of the puzzle unraveling through my mind. Melissa must have been starkly aware of the precarious nature of her discovery, enough to risk our daughter's life and take precautionary action. *Queen Avila.* I realized that my girl acted as a viral host by carrying the encoded wolf gene in her system since she was a child.

Holy shit.

I had created the Sanguisa with the blood taken from Shane's newborn baby girl, Shana. It was obvious that the wolf-cum-vampire creatures sniffed out the original Lygarou blood gene in Avila. My head spun as I began to understand that even as acting as a viral host, Avila was their Alpha. Even more jarring was the fact that her blood carries the encoded gene that will cure the V-virus – the missing link needed to eradicate the undead for good. The answer to rid the earth of vampires had been in my face the entire time.

Long before the apocalypse hit, Melissa had ensured we possessed the key to reverse the damage caused by magic and genetic mutation. I loved her even more in that moment, even as I lit up on the inside as much as broke on old truths. I had made so many mistakes that had cost the lives of innocent people. I had lived on the edge of desperation, hatred, and failure; mourned lost love and feared for my daughter. I had died and visited the other side only to return to discover that while I can't control change, I can still offer the world and my girl a chance at salvation.

My voice was almost a singsong as I started to laugh.

"Avila! You're their Alpha, girl!"

"Alpha? Huh?" The crowd broke into a chorus of gasps and chatter as I hauled myself up onto the stage and she started toward me. "How's that possible?"

"Your mother."

"Mom?" She halted. I could almost see the wheels turning in her head as she began to figure it out. "The dream messages—and the plaster?"

"Yes!"

I laughed some more and vaguely heard Marius chuckle over the perplexing rumbles emanating from the vampires on stage as they looked at one another. Some of them slapped each other's backs, the blood caking their faces spilled with laughter. Others, those who showed up for violence and slaughter, gave lowly snarls and peered at Zaros who remained remarkably silent on the far side of the stage as a thrilling vibe raptured across the blood city.

Everything was going to be okay.

I could feel it in my bones as the five Sanguisa stood up, their spindly figures turned to cast eyes on Avila, watching for her cues. They each appeared the same in that their skin clumped rotted, gritty, and brindled beneath scarcely covered scalps, and there was a coldness in their eyes that superseded any vampire I had ever seen. I shivered in the knowledge that they belonged to Avila and not Zaros, and now, his play for power was over.

It seemed that every vampire in the Crypt courtyard

started to get the gist of Avila's powerful status and the ramifications it represented. She was their vampire queen despite the Claiming hour had now passed. Marius would have no choice but to wait for the next full moon to claim my girl. That would buy me some time to start on working the secrets in her blood. This time I was determined to get it right. Buoyancy incited thunderous applause and jubilant cheers in the throng of vampires before their acclamations fused into one collective chant.

"Queen Avila! Queen Avila!"

She and Marius exchanged a smile. He gave her a nod and stepped back before she turned toward the audience, laughing. I knew she was still processing her part in all of this, but she was handling it rather well. I'd never seen her shine so bright. Her white dress illuminated heavenly against the iridescent candle flames to create an angelic impression as she took in the adoration offered by the people. I saw traces of grace and beauty borrowed by genes passed through her mother as her dark hair fell around her face when she gave a dramatic curtsey toward the audience, thanking them. Love and pride stole my heart as the crowd responded to Avila with deafening applause, but it was gone just as fast when a spine-chilling growl emanated from the side of the stage. The next thing I saw was the blood spreading over Avila's white dress and the wooden stake protruding from her heart before she collapsed.

"No—Avila!"

My voice was a strangled sound as I caught sight of Michal's grisly grin before I rushed to her side. Marius was there as I fell to my knees and yanked the stake from her chest. It clanked on the stage, but I heard nothing. *Nothing.* Sinister secrets clawed at my soul as I reached to cradle her.

"Livvie!" Marius cried out next to me, but I ignored him.

Blood leaked warm and sticky between my fingers and spread over the stage like a scarlet river. "A-Avila." Her skin hollowed against her cheekbones, fractured and ashen. I shook her gently. "Please—baby girl."

Please.

Marius stood up and growled as Sanguisa howls promised treachery and death in the night. In the next second, the five beasts were beside Michal and removing his limbs. My hair stood up as his wild screams echoed across the stage, but I felt nothing for him, vaguely recalling the innocent scientists he had murdered in cold blood before I had turned kindred. I was a fool to believe in him again. The sound of his tearing flesh and crunching bones snapped against the backdrop of splattering blood before his desperate cries stopped abruptly. My heart was a husk as I focused on Avila.

"I beg you," I told her. "Don't go from here, from me."

The assault was over. The Sanguisa had taken their retribution on my girl's attacker but her death was enough to reignite the supernatural bloodline butchery. No holds barred. The night filled with deranged screams and breaking flesh as Marius and Zaros led their men with a rage lit by the flames of hell.

I was aware of nothing but the silence of Avila's dead heart.

WAITING FOR THE DAY

y vision blurred. The veins on Avila's temples spilt like shriveled vines beneath skin that only moments before flushed with lifeforce energy. I reached for her hair. The dark brittle strands crumbled between my fingers like dried straw. She was gone. *Gone.* The acute pain radiating in my chest resisted what I didn't want to know, and yet, I couldn't deny the sight of her fast degenerating corpse.

The timber podium vibrated to the strains of stomping boots and minced bodies as vampires stalked and menaced. It was a Sanguisa meat party. The beasts had rallied with Zaros and turned on Marius' men. A dozen more Mysticus guards had spilled onto the stage to fight in the name of who knew what? Nothing mattered anymore. Blood splashed in my face as I drew my girl into my arms and shook violently.

Avila.

Amalgamation was eerie sheiks, gruesome grunts and vile snarls pinging with the dull ache in my muscles. I closed my eyes and buried my face in her neck. Her arms floundered by her sides. She smelled sooty as I spoke against her thickening skin.

"I failed you again. I-I didn't see it coming."

My shirt soaked up the last of her life and I was as dead on the inside as she was. I started to rock her limp body. "I should have been someone better for you. I-I couldn't see past my own hatred—Avila. Y-you were right, I should've tried harder to accept the new world."

I gave an unrecognizable shriek as Sun appeared, yelling over raspy breaths, swinging stakes, and slashing claws.

"Jett! We've got to get out of here now!"

I looked up. Her eyes darted, jungli. The crowd, who had cheered Avila as their queen, had mostly dispersed save for the brave who chose a side and fought with vigor. A body thumped on the timber boards next to me, vacant eyes over a gashed throat and skin like aged cheese. I became aware of heat. Flames licked the backstage curtains. Candelabras were awry as smoke gathered above like a bleak fog. Burning flesh stunk like grilling pork. Sun yanked at my collar, jarring me.

"Jett!" She was breathless. "You've no time to think about it. Let's go!"

I couldn't think, but I wasn't leaving Avila here on the

stage to become a trampled barbecued kebab. I gave a nod and stood, scooping my girl in my arms, and turning to follow Sun. I stopped short when I saw Marius facing the sharp, unremitting blows of a Sanguisa. The skin on his face broke in vermillion threads, and his attempts to ward off the monstrous vampire saw him take a fist through the stomach. His eyes bulged as the Sanguisa sniggered and played fisticuffs with his innards. Zaros charged into view, burning a path through brawling vampires to serve up a crescent kick to his jaw. Marius dropped like a bag of bones as Sun urged me forward.

"Come on!"

Damn. I hesitated. The world was nothing without my girl. Sun shook her head as I pushed Avila's body in her arms. "Take her home. I'll be right after you."

She went to protest but stopped when she saw the look in my eyes. I gave her a gentle shove, but I didn't wait to watch her leave. I whirled around with a bloodthirsty hiss before sprinting toward the Sanguisa who was now dragging Marius to his feet under Zaros' command. The overlord was about to become sausage stew.

Adrenaline felt like hot needles. I growled and launched myself on the Sanguisa's back, punching him in the neck with my right hand while piercing his throat with the other. He roared and released Marius, thrashing around hard enough to send me reeling. I hit a blood swamped floor, and Zaros was sneering in my face.

His black eyes were pitiless. "So, you've made your choice, even in the wake of her death."

He laughed. Lunacy chilled my spine. I glimpsed Marius gasping and doubled over behind him. Blood dripped from the Sanguisa's chin as he rolled his head and growled. Zaros flicked a wrist at me. "Finish him."

I had no time to move. The Sanguisa screeched. Pink saliva sprayed in my mouth as he tackled me, walloping my forehead with a rock-hard headbutt. The back of my skull banged against the stage. In the next instant, his talons tore shreds at my ears and eyes. I pushed a fist into his gut, just breaking through his shirt enough to connect with flesh. The meat of his palm shattered my elbow as he forced my hand from his chest before he pinned me down and drew back his right arm to make the deadly play for my heart. His weight was like a moving truck.

A flashing red eye.

Inhale.

Twisting lips and blood-hungry intent.

Exhale.

The battle blasted all around, ringing in my ears as the Sanguisa splayed his razor-sharps over me. I squirmed and reached into my pocket to grasp Sun's crystal energy wand. I barely glimpsed Marius and Zaros as they growled and caged one another, going at it head to head.

Inhale.

The mutated creature crabbed his fingers and roared as he went to penetrate my ribcage, and at the same time,

I roared and stabbed the wand into his throat with a force that surprised me.

Exhale.

The Sanguisa gurgled. His thick tongue hung from his mouth as his eyes expelled yellow pussy gunk and he grappled for the wand that was buried in his neck. I shoved him off me and rolled out from beneath him. He started to gasp for air and writhe as I stood over him.

"Motherfucker," I said as I smashed my boot into his head. His skull cracked and caved in, and I became aware of Zaros as he shouted from some place behind me.

"Sanguisa!"

His next command was snuffed by the stake Marius speared through his chest. His face conveyed utter shock while a flood of Mysticus guards converged onto the stage. Zaros thudded heavily to the floor. His bloody talons wrapped around the stake and he spluttered. He opened his mouth to say something, producing blood instead. Then the surviving Sanguisa were at his side, their shoulders hunched as they stalked around him protectively. His other crew members left alive rallied together and fled from the scene.

Zaros' eyes rolled back. He groaned as Draven Sanguisa gathered him up, nursing him not unlike a mother nurses her child. The cold-blooded beast took his weight easily. His demonic eyes flashed, and his neck elongated with a drawn-out hiss as the guards barraged forward. A thousand footsteps pounded behind me.

His voice was something from the netherworld.

"Waiting for the day, doc."

I clenched my fists but said nothing as he lurched around, moving as if part of an incorporeal realm before he took off with Zaros, his fellow creatures following him from the stage.

Every vampire left standing remained silent. I didn't look around at the carnage left from the supernatural clash my daughter's death had incited. I didn't even look at Marius as he came up next to me, watching the Sanguisa disappear into the night. Their formless prints belonged to the shadows and went unheard, and the silence was broken by the occasional howl as the distance between us stretched.

Numbness took hold and I went to leave. Marius stopped me.

"Jett."

I wiped my brow and looked at him.

"Why?" he said.

"Because despite everything, the world would be that much worse without you." My voice cracked. "And you loved my daughter."

He gave a nod. "I'm sorry, Jett."

I nodded and he gestured at the Sanguisa left behind. The one I'd killed with Sun's wand. His body had deflated like a fossilized relic. A wilted version of a creature that shouldn't exist. Marius shook his head.

"How did you kill him?"

"I guess I uncovered their weakness."

"What?"

"Silver."

I started to walk away, and he called out after me.

"Where are you going?"

My heart seized in a violent implosion. I stopped walking but didn't turn around when I answered. "I'm going to wait for the day."

The day of Ascension.

THE END

Dear reader, thank you for your valuable time. Did you enjoy this book? Please consider leaving your review at Amazon.com

ABOUT KIM PETERSEN

Author. Writer. Dreamer. Beautiful Delusions. Lover of coffee, summer storms, great books, the mystical, soul & people with heart – Come fly with me.
Kim Petersen is a *USA Today Bestselling* author of the new *Blood Legends* series, *The Ascended Angels Chronicles*, and co-author of the *Stone the Crows* series. Her debut novel, *Millie's Angel* received a gold award in the 2017 Dan Poynter's Global eBook Awards.

Subscribe to Kim's fiction newsletter to keep in touch

CONTACT

Website: http://bit.ly/kimpetersen
Facebook: http://bit.ly/2MdNLjK
Twitter: https://twitter.com/kimpetersen_
Amazon: https://amzn.to/2APcSF0
Bookbub: http://bit.ly/2Tt8weC